THE WANDERING TRAILS

The Wandering Trails

Esther Loewen Vogt

HORIZON BOOKS
CAMP HILL, PENNSYLVANIA

Horizon Books
3825 Hartzdale Drive
Camp Hill, PA 17011

ISBN: 0-87509-103-5
LOC Catalog Card Number: 93-74957
© 1994 by Christian Publications
Printed in the United States of America

94 95 96 97 98 5 4 3 2 1

Cover illustration by Brenda Wintermyer
Cover design by Step One Design

DEDICATION

To my son Ranney Vogt whose loving, congenial, Christ-like spirit, like Willie's, is a constant joy and blessing to me!

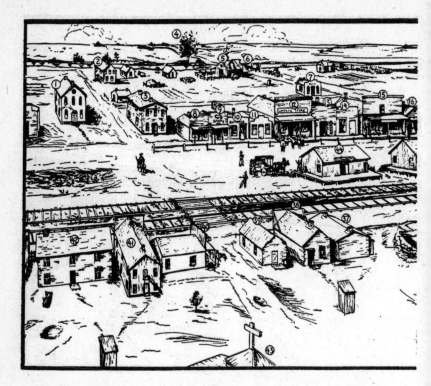

This drawing by Bernard Wardlow is an outline of the early business district of Ellsworth in 1871. The names and types of buildings pictured represent the best reconstruction that could be made from descriptions provided by Charles Larkin and early files of *The Ellsworth Reporter.*

1–Hotel 2–Two-story house (used fictiously as Barbara and Charlie Warren's house in the story) 3–Two-story house 4–Hangman's tree south of the present bridge across the river 5–Livery Stable on the banks of the river 6–Smoky Hill River wagon and cattle crossing 7–Small hotel 8–Joe Brennan's Saloon 9–Nick Lent's Saloon 10–Butcher Shop 11–Gambling joint 12–Larkin's General Store 13–Hank's Barber Shop 14–Beebe's General Merchandise Store 15–The American House (hotel) 16–Store 17–Ringolsky's Store 18–Store

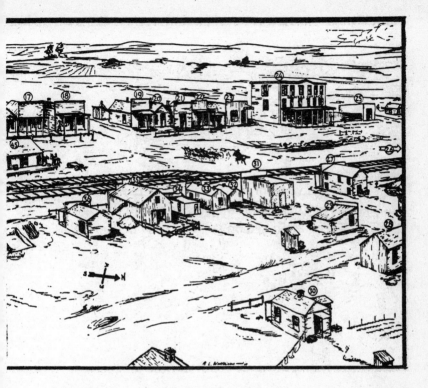

19–Hoesman's Hardware Store 20–Store 21–Doctor's Office 22–Restaurant 23–Shoe Shop 24–The Cottage Hotel (aka Drover's Cottage) 25–Livery Stable 26–the direction of the stock yards about 200 yards north of the tracks 27–Hotel 28–Episcopal Church 29–Nunamaker's Jewelry Store 30–House (now First Street) 31–Seitz Drugstore 32–Schmitt's Shoe Store 33–Herzig's Grocery Store 34–Saloon 35–Livery Stable, Hay Barn and Corral 36–Larkin's Store 37–Bowling Alley 38–Beech's Hotel and Post Office 39–Larkin's Store 40–Grand Central Hotel 41–*The Reporter* Office 42–Court House 43–Catholic Church 44–Kansas Pacific Railroad Depot 45–Freight Depot.

(Reprinted with the permission of *The Ellsworth Reporter*.)

AUTHOR'S NOTE

*F*or readers like me who like to have the fact and fiction sorted out, I offer the following:

At the beginning, the Smoky Hill was a dangerous route to the West. It was considered the shortest and most direct trail through the wilderness, to what was once called The Great American Desert. Beyond beckoned the gold fields of the mountains, trade in New Mexico, or a free land for new homes for settlers. As other parts of the West became the focal points for the traveler, many trails sprung up and wandered across the Plains. The Smoky Hill Trail (sometimes called the "Starvation Trail") snaked along the river that bears its name. Yet the entire Plains country was a battleground as hostile Indians plagued wagon trains, freighters, and stagecoaches that dared cross this fertile country.

When settlement of the country began, it naturally appeared along the trails where travelers stopped and settled down, often forming the nucleus for a town. Here, along this trail and the Smoky Hill River, the town of Ellsworth took root in 1867.

The beginnings of Ellsworth were troubled ones. Natural disasters dogged this fledgling town set along the western edge of the Fort Harker Military Reservation. Still, the fort offered protection and the Smoky Hill River nearby provided a ready water supply. After a flood, the town relocated a few miles upstream. When the railroad came, hopes rose for establishing a major cattle market and brought in many respectable business people, as well as gamblers, thieves, gunmen, prostitutes and other "riffraff." By 1873 Ellsworth had a reputation as the "wickedest town in the West." By then the Indians no longer bothered the settlers.

This is the setting where fictitious characters Charlie and Barbara Warren, their two small sons, and Charlie's congenial teenaged brother Willie had moved in 1872. It was ideal ranch country, although the fresh start the Warrens hoped to achieve soon turned into disaster. The Texas cattle that crossed the prairie into Kansas were first headed toward Abilene, Kansas where the nearest railroad was located. After the Kansas Pacific Railroad reached Ellsworth, the town lured the Texas longhorn cattle trade to the Cox Trail, or "Ellsworth Cattle Trail," which shortened the trip from Texas to the market by three days. Thirty-five miles were saved by using this fork off the Chisholm Trail.

As the cattle trade increased, so did violence in Ellsworth; fist-fights, gunfights, and drunken brawls were common. The most notable incident of 1873 was the killing of Sheriff Whitney on August 15 when he tried to break up a fight. The mix of alcohol and poker was no doubt the cause of the fracas.

At one time historical figures such as William F. ("Buffalo Bill") Cody, Wild Bill Hickok, and Wyatt Earp lived briefly in the town or visited it.

There is some controversy about the episode of Wyatt Earp in the tragic skirmish between Sheriff Whitney and the Thompsons, yet many believed that it did happen. It was in Ellsworth that Earp made his start as a peace officer, and from then on his fame grew.

In spite of the town's wickedness, several churches took a stand for morality and Christianity, with Rev. Levi Sternberg as one of its pioneer pastors.

Before the summer of 1873 a severe drought hit the Plains. Then the eastern cattle market collapsed with the decline of the New York Stock Exchange. This resulted in the demise of the cattle industry.

After the dust storms of 1873, a prairie fire swept across the Plains. But by 1876 the town overcame its tragedies and had settled down to peace and quiet, despite several major fires that gutted parts of the town from time to time. The aforementioned events are based on facts and are an actual part of Ellsworth's background.

It is in this setting I place Barbara Warren and her family. I have tried to portray this era of Ellsworth history (1872-73) and its wandering trails through Barbara's eyes. If it has deviated from fact, it is no less stranger than the facts themselves, which were sometimes vague and unclear in my research. Thus, this novel is a work of fiction, but based on fact and used fictitiously.

Esther Loewen Vogt
Hillsboro, Kansas

"When you pass through the waters,
   I will be with you;
and when you pass through the rivers,
   they will not sweep over you.
When you walk through the fire,
   you will not be burned;
   the flames will not set you ablaze.
For I am the LORD, your God,
   the Holy One of Israel, Your Savior."
      (Isaiah 43:2–3a, NIV)

CHAPTER 1

The valley of the Smoky Hill nestles in the palm of the vast Kansas prairie, and along this strip of fertile farmland sprawls the river which bears its name. The Smoky Hill Trail stretches ahead over this treeless plain where bent or broken stems of wiry grass and crushed flowers cover indistinct wagon ruts pointing the way to Ellsworth.

For days the covered wagon had creaked and clanked along the Trail from Cottonwood Crossing. The woman seated on the high seat gazed toward the grassy horizon that dipped and swelled in the late afternoon. She pushed back her pink, faded sunbonnet and turned to the man seated beside her, the reins hanging loosely from his hands.

"Oh, Charlie," she cried out suddenly, "will this be a good place to live?"

"Ellsworth?" The team slowed as the reins relaxed and he turned toward her. "You've weathered these past five years at the Crossing, Barbara, and you'll weather this, too. My job as foreman at the Wilcox Ranch is just what I need. Lucky for you and the boys, Willie and I already drove our cattle down to the spread to spare you from the hot, smelly dust of all those hooves." He paused and peered anxiously at her tired face. "You all right?"

Barbara smiled a little, her lustrous blue eyes crinkling at the corners. She was exhausted, but Charlie Warren wouldn't find it out from her if she could help it. She felt gritty and dusty from the five days of this journey.

"I'll be glad to reach that funny little town and stretch my legs. I'm surprised the boys have been so quiet back there." She turned and glanced to the rear of the wagon where the boys were napping in the shade of the canvas cover of the wagon. A dozen or so round, prickly globes from the Osage hedges near the stage stop lay scattered on their laps and on the floor of the wagon.

"Danny's usually up here with me, you know," Charlie said, pushing his sweaty felt hat back from his dark curls, "but I told him he had to take care of his little brother until we got to our new place. I gave them a bunch of hedge balls to play with. Keeps them busy."

Wearily Barbara pulled the bonnet down toward her forehead and closed her eyes. The six years at Cottonwood had been rough, but good, years. In fact, the past eight years had been the strangest, yet the most happy years of her life. Had it been only nine years since she, Barbara Temple, had left her home in Atlanta to live in Kansas with her Uncle Daniel Moore and his family in 1863?

After her marriage to Charlie Warren in 1865, they had lived for a year on the lonely plains of Western Kansas—until hostile Indians had stormed along the Santa Fe Trail. Barbara had escaped the horror of that raid when she and her cousin Elizabeth Moore had gone to Atlanta in August of 1866 to pursue the possibility of her inheriting her Uncle Alex Temple's plantation. Her hopes for the inheritance were dashed when she learned they'd have to move to Georgia and live on the plantation in order to gain ownership. She knew Charlie would never leave Kansas.

Their two sons, Daniel Charles and Jeremy David, were born in a one-room shanty near the stage stop at the Crossing some 60 miles to the southeast. Danny was almost six now, and Jem had just turned two. She was expecting their third child in March.

Now it was 1872 and they were moving to the frontier prairie town of Ellsworth. Since there was no house for them near the ranch, Charlie had rented a clapboard, two-story dwelling in town. Barbara looked forward to the more spacious living quarters. The two rooms downstairs and two rooms upstairs would seem roomy compared to their tiny stone shack at the Crossing or the sodhouse they occupied out West. Charlie and his 18-year-old brother, Willie, had already driven their small herd of cattle to the Wilcox spread several weeks ago. Their dozen head of cattle had merged with the herd at the Wilcox ranch. Charlie would ride five miles every day to work on horseback.

The creak of wagon wheels, the faint clank of harness and the swish of horse hooves through the deep prairie growth was a scene etched on Barbara's mind from their earlier wanderings. The aroma of crushed grass had been bringing back those memories all week long. Now her eyes strained ahead, eager to catch a glimpse of their new home. Ellsworth boasted a population of 1,300. The Kansas-Missouri Railroad had pushed across the prairies and had reached the town two years earlier. At least it wouldn't be as lonely as their little soddy in Western Kansas, she hoped.

Charlie worked at Lank Moore's ranch at Cottonwood Crossing for the past six years. He had recently accepted the job as foreman on the Dick Wilcox spread south of Ellsworth where they were now headed. Within the hour they would arrive at the new house.

The Trail wound around the shoulder of a low hill, and wandered westward. Barbara knew that the town had an unusual main street divided by the tracks of the railroad. Buildings with businesses faced the grade and rails from both sides of the wide street. There was plenty of room to drive teams and wagons between the tracks and the business sections.

Now as the wagon lumbered toward town, Barbara could make out the tracks snaking from the east down its very center.

They drove through the shallow Smoky Hill River, crossing with scarcely a ripple where many wagons and cattle had passed before. Along the dusty main street squatted three blocks of businesses from shops to saloons. Charlie had told her there were plenty of hotels, rooming houses and bordellos, and now she was seeing some of them with her own eyes. Charlie turned the team onto a side street heading south and pointed to a two-story structure a short distance ahead on the right.

"There it is, Barbara. Our home."

It was a crude, ugly, unpainted frame building, with a front door cut into the east side and small lean-to and sheds in the rear. The bare windows gaped back at her. She gulped a little. *What had I expected? Not this shabby gray structure. But at least it's bigger than the shanty at the Crossing.*

Already the sun had lowered in the west and was dipping toward the horizon. A small breeze had sprung up, cooling the sultry September afternoon.

With Charlie's stiff "Whoa!" the team stopped at the front door. As he helped her from the wagon, Barbara paused and half-listened for Shanghai Pierce's bullhorn voice, which they said could be heard all over town when he spoke. Pierce was a Texas cattleman who was bringing his herds of longhorns to the railroads in Kansas.

"They claim when he whispers, you can hear it a half mile away," Willie had told her. "He's noisier than a circus calliope with a voice more piercin' than a train whistle!"

Barbara stretched herself languidly while Charlie helped the two boys from the rear of the wagon. Jem leaned over to pick up a few of the hedge balls that had tumbled to the ground.

Immediately tow-headed Danny rushed toward the door, with a wide grin splitting his freckled face.

"Oh, Momma, is this gonna be our home?"

Barbara paused to scoop Jem into her arms. "So your papa tells me. Look at all the room we'll have."

"Me want water." Jem squirmed impatiently until Barbara

4

set him back on the ground.

"Soon, Jem. Papa will get a fresh pailful as soon as he can."

Charlie had already unlocked the door and stood in the doorway with his arms akimbo. "Do you want me to escort you into your palatial quarters, ma'am?" he said as he waited with an impish grin. "It's not much yet, Barbara, but after we get our things in—"

"Hey, Barbara." Willie leaned down from his horse as he rode up. "You remember when we moved into the soddy near Pawnee Rock, how Mame Probst came to take charge? She put all our stuff where *she* wanted. I remember how it riled you somethin' fierce. Well, do you think you could use Mame now?"

"How can I ever forget Mame?" Barbara said softly, leaning her head against Charlie's shoulder. "Gritty as sandpaper and snappy as a turtle. But yes, I wish she were here! Now show me our home, Charlie."

"After you, my dear."

He followed her indoors. The kitchen was fairly large, although with scant furnishings. The double walls were made of wood painted an ugly lead-colored gray. A bare table made of cottonwood planks, a rusty black cookstove, two empty nail kegs, two broken chairs, a coffee grinder screwed onto the wall and a few other utensils comprised the kitchen. A bed and a battered chest were in the bedroom to the north. A rickety set of stairs led to the opening that yawned above them. There were neither curtains nor blinds on the windows, nor rugs on the floor nor pictures on the walls. She frowned.

"Sure looks like ya could use Mame," Willie repeated, peering at the bare, primitive rooms. "But in time you'll fix things up fine. And put things where *you* want 'em!"

Barbara felt the rush of weariness sweep over her again and she sat down on one of the crude nail kegs. Jem toddled toward her and threw himself into her arms. *I'm almost too tired to hold him,* she thought. *I need to fix something to eat, but I can't seem to move.*

She leaned her head back against the wall and closed her

eyes. Then she heard Charlie and Willie slamming around with pots and pans.

Jem began to fret and whimper. Barbara knew he was tired and thirsty. She tried to stagger to her feet holding Jem, but she was too exhausted.

"Wait, Jem."

She cuddled him gently, and then set him down. Willie was already stirring up a batch of biscuits while Charlie struggled with a fire in the rusty old range.

"Just rest awhile, Barbara," he called over his shoulder. "This stove may take a bit of coaxing. I'll get the hang of it yet. You're pretty beat, aren't you?"

She didn't say anything. It took almost too much effort to speak. Jem was crying now, and she picked him up and held him close. "You want a drink, don't you, Honey? Maybe Uncle Willie will get a bucket of water for us now." She looked up as Willie shoved the panful of biscuits into the oven. "And would you please take Danny with you?" she called out when he started for the door.

"We have to go to the town pump," Willie said. Picking up the wooden pails from the corner, he slammed out of the house with Danny trotting after him.

Charlie's fire snapped and crackled as it blazed on the grate. Then he took a skillet and sliced strips of bacon into it. Soon it sputtered, its aroma filling the hot, stuffy room. Barbara got up and stood in the doorway to catch a breath of air, and stroked Jem's tawny hair with aching arms. She remembered how sick she'd been before Danny was born. It was when she and Cousin Bitsy had been in Atlanta that the doctor had told her she was going to have a baby. At first she had been upset. Babies often died on the prairie, and she wasn't sure she wanted a child. But things had gone well with both boys. Now she felt the same utter weariness she had fought before Danny was born. Of course, the five-day wagon trip hadn't helped.

"Is there dried corn in that tin?" Charlie asked as he rummaged through a crate he brought from the wagon. "I recall we packed all the dried stuff in those big lard cans."

She nodded. "And add a dollop of butter if it isn't rancid."

Just then she looked out at the dusty street. Willie was balancing two pails of water as Danny skipped along beside him, his face creased with a smudgy grin. He broke into a run and called out.

"Momma, we seed lots of bad men with dirty faces and black hats. They come bustin' out of the—what did you call it, Uncle Willie?"

"Saloon, Danny. It's not a very nice place. I hope you'll always stay out of them." He pushed through the doorway with the water.

"S-saloon? The pump is near a saloon?" Barbara stammered. Of course, she'd been warned that Ellsworth was a rough town, but she'd tried to push the thought from her mind. This was to be their home, and she wanted it to be pleasant.

"One of a dozen saloons, not to mention hotels, bordellos and boardin' houses. Yup, this town won't be dull," he said, setting the water pails in one corner, "if ya crave excitement."

"Well, I don't! I hope we can keep away from the rough element," Barbara said in a thin voice. "We'll have as little to do with them as we can."

Willie placed his hands on his hips. "That won't be as easy as it sounds. But I've just been offered a job in the lumberyard. I'll still haul all the water ya need, Barbara, so you won't have to go out to the pump often. Maybe you can avoid the town," he said with a grin.

"That's . . . that is nice of you, Willie. I'd hoped it wouldn't be so lonely here. But with the saloons and dance halls—"

"Oh! I almost forgot to tell you. There's also a small congregation that meets in a little stone building at Thompson's Creek. They're mostly farmers and ranchers who come. And guess who the parson is? Reverend Levi Sternberg!"

Barbara let out a small gasp. The very thought of a worship service conducted by a preacher who had once visited them at Pawnee Rock gave her a lift. She poured a dipper full of water into a tin cup and gave it to Jem, who gulped it greedily.

"Not so fast, Jem. Take it more slowly. Well, maybe this place won't be so bad after all," she added.

"Kin I go with Willie when he gets more water, Momma?" Danny begged, excitement dancing in his blue eyes. "I like to see the horses and the *twains*, and those mean, bad men that go yelling in the s'loon!"

"It's trains, dear," she said mechanically.

Her heart constricted with a sudden fear. Was this an omen? *Oh, dear God, please take care of us here as You've done in the past!* she prayed silently.

CHAPTER 2

*I*n a little while the Warrens were settled into the drafty clapboard house. Although the rooms were quite spacious, the house lacked the cozy comfort of their sodhouse in Western Kansas. The double walls were drab and unplastered, and Barbara almost wished for the unpalatable clay mixed with manure that had covered the walls of the soddy. When whitewashed to a glistening, sugary white, the mixture made a durable attractive interior. But she couldn't ask Charlie or Willie to do it now. The south room had become a sort of kitchen/dining/living room, while the one to the north served as bedroom for Barbara and Charlie and the boys, who shared a trundle bed. Willie slept upstairs in the south room with the low ceiling.

He had grown into a lanky teenager of 18 these past six years. He was 10 when she had first met him. After his sister, Nellie May, and their parents had been killed by Indians on their way to Kansas in 1862, Charlie had tried to make a home for his congenial, freckle-faced young brother near Marion Centre.

Willie had been the first real friend Barbara had made when she came to live with her Uncle Daniel Moore and his family, who lived across the Cottonwood River. She learned that she could count on Willie in any situation. She had nursed him faithfully when he was so desperately ill with diphtheria that first fall, and he never forgot it.

Even when he came home tired from his job at the lumberyard, he still found time to play with Danny and Jem, which relieved Barbara of their care. A jumble of thoughts whirled through her mind as she sat at the rickety table and pared potatoes for their evening meal. What would she ever do without him?

Just then, he swung into the kitchen and sailed his hat into the far corner of the room.

"I figured you needed more water," he said, snitching a slice of raw potato from the panful in Barbara's lap. "Let me take the little fellers with me and get them outta your hair for a spell."

"Oh, would you?" Barbara brightened. "Jem's been fussy all day. He's too young to understand why we've moved to this new town. Yet Danny seems to thrive on the constant action down the street."

Willie picked a straw from the new broom in the corner and chewed on it thoughtfully. "He'll get over it—and I hope the town will, too. I wish Charlie wasn't always so tired when he comes home after managin' the ranch all day. But that's the way it is," he shrugged.

Barbara sighed and pushed back the tendrils that feathered around her face. "I know. Still, I'm thankful he has steady work, and he seems to like it. And with the prospect of raising our cattle along with Dick Wilcox's herds . . . it makes sense. Luckily he has Sundays off. That was one stipulation he made, you know."

Willie grabbed his hat with one hand and the water pails with the other. "Yep. It's good to be near a real church, too, although ain't too many folks comin' yet. You made any friends with the ladies around here?"

Barbara laughed. "Not really. The people at church are mostly from farms and ranches, as you said, and I haven't visited the bordellos and dance halls looking for others."

"Well, one of these days you'll meet some."

"Dance hall dolls or other female characters?" she called out after him as he headed out of the house. Barbara heard him call to Danny and Jem.

She got ponderously to her feet and stirred the fire in the rusty black range. It was larger than the little topsy stove they'd had in the soddy, but she had to admit that the tiny topsy stove had served them well. Of course, for a larger, draftier house this old stove was necessary.

Stirring up the inevitable panful of cornbread, she heard squeals of laughter as Willie returned with the water and the two small boys in tow.

"We seed the twain—train—come in, but Jem was scared of it," Danny said with a brave-brother grin. "Did you see it, Momma?"

Willie set the pails of water in their corner and turned to Barbara. "Why don't you take a look at that train? You don't get out all day, do you? I'll look after the little fellers for ya."

"See the train? What's so special about seeing a train, Willie?"

"Oh, nothin'. But you need a change of scene. Go on!"

It was true. She had hardly left the house since they had settled in only two weeks before, except to take the boys out to play now and then. Without a word, she snatched the faded pink bonnet from its nail behind the door and jammed it on her head. *I'm almost too tired,* she told herself, *but I do need a break.*

With a wave of her hand she walked out of the house and started up the dusty street that led north to the wide main street. The town reminded her of a mole on the jaw of the broad valley. Already the sun was slipping behind the horizon and she hurried, her shoes kicking up skiffs of dirt. She could see the business places that faced the tracks, with their wooden awnings shading the board sidewalks. New stores and saloons were springing up everywhere around the plaza. A haze of dust sifted over the streets from the constant stream of horse-drawn vehicles that rattled up and down.

In front of the butcher shop, Barbara paused. She could see

the dingy little depot from where she stood. The engine was still chuffing and its valves were popping with steam. It was good to know that the train could take passengers where they needed to go. A few women clustered outside the station, probably waiting for the train to leave for Denver. Most of the Indians had gone on to their reservations and there was little danger on the plains from them now. Yet she sensed something raw and restless on the dusty streets of this frontier town, and she gave an involuntary shudder.

Just then a young women stumbled out of the Lent's Saloon next to the butcher shop with her long brown hair disheveled and her dark red, watered-silk skirt mussed and dirty.

"Why don'cha watch where y're goin', Nance Drubeck?" A man's angry voice muttered. "You ought to stick to your job and get outta a man's way!" A soldier from Fort Harker pushed her roughly aside.

Nance Drubeck! The name rang like a familiar bell in Barbara's memory. Then she remembered. It was Mame Probst's niece who had some sort of job in Ellsworth.

Nance looked sullen with hard lines creeping around her pretty bow-shaped mouth, but somehow the green eyes reminded Barbara of a frightened rabbit. As the girl whirled toward the door of the saloon, Barbara impulsively grabbed the thin, white arm.

"You're—Nance? Mame Probst's niece?" she began hesitantly. "Can you tell me what's happened to Mame?"

Nance jerked away from Barbara's hand. "Well, who wants to know? And who cares?" Her thick, slurred voice rose shrilly.

"Mame—Mame was our neighbor once. One of the best people I ever met," Barbara went on boldly. "And I'm Barbara Warren."

The girl eyed her shrewdly, like a cat watching a mouse. "So why do you want to know? I doubt Aunt Mame is your type. I can see you're one of them high-falutin' dames who thinks she's too good to neighbor with us—prostitutes. What's Aunt Mame told you about me?" The gaze narrowed.

Barbara stepped back. Did she really want to have anything

to do with this—riffraff? But if she was Mame's niece ... After what Mame had done for them at Pawnee Rock, she wanted to do something in return.

"Nance, I haven't seen Mame in over five years, and all she ever said was that you worked in a dance hall. Can you tell me what's happened to her?"

Nance drew back, her facial muscles softening. "Well, she never had much use for me. Nobody does. Last I heard, Aunt Mame was at Fort Dodge. Guess she's still fixin' grub for eatin' houses. Now, will ya leave me alone?" She tried to push past but Barbara kept a hand on her arm.

"Nance, I learned to love your aunt when she proved to be a real friend to me at Pawnee Rock. She was rough and bossy, but underneath all of that, she had a heart of gold. And for her sake, if I can help you in any way—"

"Don't need your help. Don't want it, neither." She shrugged from Barbara's grip and started back for the saloon.

"Wait." Barbara reached out her arm again. "Nance, I'd like to—to be your friend if you're ever in some sort of trouble."

"Who says I'm in trouble?" Nance's green eyes grew hard again, and her voice sharp. "Hah! If you're one of them goody-goodies like some of them church folk I've met, I don't need you. What does God care about somebody like me anyhow?"

There it was again. The scared look in Nance's green eyes. She whirled around and slammed into the saloon.

Slowly Barbara turned and started toward the house. She felt deflated. *I really shouldn't care what Nance does. And yet, I wish she'd at least talk to me. But why I should care about a prostitute who doesn't want anything to do with me, I don't know.*

As she hurried down the street, the sweetness of the autumn evening fell over the town, hiding its ugliness and smoothing its raw outlines. A bobwhite called from somewhere in the twilight that was creeping over the prairies, and she walked faster. She knew Charlie would be riding in from the ranch any minute, and it was time to put the cornbread into the oven and fry the potatoes.

She sighed again. *Well, I tried,* she told herself. *I wanted to be nice to Nance, but she wants nothing from me.*

She spread out her hands helplessly as she stepped across the threshold into the kitchen, grateful for the comfort and love of her little family.

CHAPTER 3

*O*ctober had turned crisp, with a chill in the air. Fields were umbered with dead cornstalks and pastures shaded from mauve to pale tan. Dove-gray skies hung low with the approach of winter, and a low wind keened along the Smoky Hill River. Already ducks and geese were headed south in V-shapes as they clacked and shrieked overhead.

Although the fire in the range burned briskly, the bare windows were drab with a too-early darkness.

Barbara stirred the beef stew once more, and glanced at the Seth Thomas clock ticking away on its little shelf where she had set it when she unpacked. Shoving the pot to the rear of the range, she spooned honey into the applesauce. She had tried to stretch the last cut of beef by fixing stew, for it seemed there was never enough money to buy what they needed.

The supper table was set, and the boys sat playing on the floor with scraps of wood Willie had brought from the lumberyard. He had just gone out with the ever-empty water pails, and Barbara waited impatiently to brew barley coffee.

Just then she heard Charlie's horse galloping toward the small barn, and she breathed a sigh of relief. He was gone from dawn until dusk, and she was always glad to see him return home.

As Willie returned with the water, Charlie stomped in after

him. His usual placid face was furrowed with worry lines.

"Charlie! Is anything wrong?" Barbara asked in alarm.

He drew off his shabby felt hat and shrugged out of his jacket. "I don't know yet. But we're facing trouble." He washed his hands and face in the gray enameled basin and dried himself with a quick swipe of the roller towel.

"What . . . what kind of trouble?" Barbara ventured, a sinking feeling at the pit of her stomach, "Indians?"

He shook his head. "No. Most of them have settled on the reservations. The fort's job may soon be over. But Abilene's cattle market is facing woes. Farmers are crowding onto the good land and plowing up the grass and fencing out cattle. So some Texas cattlemen, like Shanghai Pierce, have already been driving their longhorns to Ellsworth."

"But why? And why does that spell trouble? After all, with the Kansas-Missouri railroad—"

"But the railroad hasn't reached Texas yet. They're trompin' all over the ranch lands," Willie cut in, tousling Jem's hair, "destroying the ranch pastures, and drinkin' up water holes for domestic animals. I been hearin' complaints about this for weeks now."

Charlie sat down at the table and tapped his fork absently on his plate. "Not to mention splenic fever they're bringing in from Texas! What's that going to mean for our ranches? They figure thousands of cattle are already moving in. That can't bode much good for any of the ranches."

Barbara set the food on the table and went after the boys. "Danny and Jem, it's time to eat supper."

"I wanted to finish my stockyards first," Danny said crossly, "but Jem's always messin' it up."

"Not now. Your father and Uncle Willie are waiting. You can play after we've eaten."

Jem fussed and fretted at the table, and Barbara wound up spooning milk and cornbread into his mouth. It was a losing battle, for he spat out more than he swallowed.

In desperation she picked him up, wiped his face, and carried him into the bedroom.

"You finish your supper, Danny!" she called out over her shoulder. With a sigh she undressed Jem and pulled on his unbleached nightshirt. He whimpered, and she crooned softly as she tucked him into the trundle bed, covering him with a worn blanket. At last he settled down.

"There, there," she soothed. "Now you can go to sleep. Good night, Honey." With a light kiss on his cheek, she left the room and closed the door.

Charlie and Willie had already finished their meal and pushed back their chairs when she returned to the kitchen. Danny was playing in his corner again.

She was almost too tired to finish her plate of stew, swimming with bits of carrots and turnips and chunks of beef, but she needed to keep up her strength. *My life has certainly changed from what I dreamed it would be,* she mused.

Years ago she'd planned to marry Matthew Potter and live in a modest cottage in Atlanta. That was before the Civil War broke out and her parents and her brother, Whatley, had died, and she'd come to live in Kansas with her Uncle Daniel Moore's family. Then Matthew was killed. Soon afterward, she had found the Lord, and discovered she loved Charlie Warren, and they'd been married. Now she was a frowsy, tired, frontier woman, her hands scaly and rough, keeping house in a drafty dwelling in a rowdy town where she hadn't found a single friend.

"Why so quiet, Barbara?" Charlie interrupted her musing. She jerked up her head, scarcely aware that the stew had grown cold and the beans were congealing into an unpalatable mass on her plate.

"Oh," she said with a little gasp. "It's been a rough day and I—" Tears started rolling down her cheeks and she wiped them away with the back of her hand.

"And me dumping all of my troubles on you isn't helping matters any," Charlie said with a frown. "I'm sorry, Barbara. I keep forgetting that I've dragged you away from your old life, and now I've saddled you with more woes. If there was only something I could do to make it easier."

He looked so dejected that her heart melted. *If I didn't love him so much,* she told herself, *I would be angry with him.*

A wan smile touched her lips. "It . . . it's because I'm expecting a child that I'm so everlastingly tired. Everything— is so mixed up. And now this cattle trouble." She paused, then went on. "Tell me more about the problem with the Texas stock. What do you think will happen?"

"You gotta face it," Willie said, clearing the dirty dishes from the table. He grabbed a stump of pencil and sketched where Ellsworth and Abilene were located in Kansas in relation to neighboring Texas. "Of the two cattle towns in Kansas, Ellsworth's closer to the Texas ranges than Abilene. They tell me Ellsworth's tried to lure the cattle market from Abilene for the past two years. They're even enlargin' the stockyards west of town. We're sellin' them lots of lumber to do the job. And ol' Shanghai Pierce is determined to ship his stock out of Ellsworth. Claims there's too many grangers at Abilene, and it's gettin' mighty lawless."

"Well, it's the business people who're pushing it here," Charlie added. "It makes the town boom and that's what they want. But the local stockmen are opposed. It's bringing in more saloons and gambling dens to town. They talk about 'Godless Abilene,' but before this is over, Ellsworth will be even worse!"

Barbara toyed with her bowl of cold stew. "Not to mention dance halls. I could almost feel sorry for Nance Drubeck, except she says she doesn't need me or anyone else."

"Well, forget about Nance. You offered your friendship and she rejected it. She chose her way of life." Charlie got up and stoked the fire that flared up with a burst of warmth.

"But you didn't see how scared she looked, Charlie," Barbara said, getting up from her chair, "almost like a frightened rabbit. I wish I could tell her that God loves her. But she won't listen."

"Her kind never do," responded Charlie. "Well, after the rest of the Texas cattle here are sold, maybe some of the saloons and bordellos will close, that is, if the cattle sell."

"Why won't they sell?" Barbara asked as she wrapped the leftover cornbread in a clean cloth.

"They're in poor shape," Willie replied, plunging his hands into the pan filled with dirty dishes. "They don't sell that way. The Kansas City market don't want 'em."

"And that's what we're having to deal with," Charlie said, drawing off his cracked dusty boots. "They're here, waiting to be marketed, but since that's not happening very fast, they're left to forage for themselves. Then they trample down the good grass.

"I never seem to make the right move. Maybe we should've stayed at Marion Centre after we got married," he added somberly as he looked down at the floor. "But I had lost all those sheep when the Cottonwood flooded. Then I dragged you along to Western Kansas to that sodhouse. Then we lost everything to Indians! I'd so hoped to make a fresh start here. But with money so scarce these days . . ." His voice trailed off.

He looked up at Barbara and mustered a faint smile. Barbara smiled back demurely, then lowered her eyes.

"Here." Willie drew out his shabby wallet and placed a handful of bills on the table. "A share of my earnings." He turned to Barbara. "If you wasn't so overworked already, I could get you a roomer. Clell Dobbs over at the drugstore told me he'd like to board in a private home. He's a decent sort who don't hanker to stay in the boardin' house downtown."

"That's exactly what I'll do, Willie," Barbara said. "Feeding one extra mouth won't take that much more work. The boys need shoes, and we'll need more blankets this winter with this house so drafty. And Charlie, your boots are worn to shreds."

"No, you won't, Barbara," Charlie said quickly. "You've enough to do."

"We'll see," Barbara said slowly, with a smile.

"If it's fancy trappings you want, try Goldsoll's Store," Willie chuckled. "He's sellin' fancy clothes, boots, guns and ammunition. Even watches."

"Who needs fancy?" Barbara retorted. She knew Beebe's General Store prices were lower. Walking wearily across the room, she took Danny's arm.

"Off to bed with you, son," she said quietly. "You can play all day tomorrow—and help Momma look after Jem."

He yawned and only half-protested as he scampered into the bedroom. Barbara had lit the lamp and the bedroom flickered with eerie shadows. She had almost refused the money from Willie, for he helped her so much with hauling water and bringing in wood. She thought he ought to save his money for his own future. But when she saw Charlie's tattered boots, she knew they needed the extra cash.

If I didn't feel so very tired, she told herself for the hundredth time. *How'll I ever carry this baby until next March?* She went to the window and looked out. The same yellow cowslip moon that she had seen since coming to the Kansas prairie sailed bravely in the dark, cold winter sky.

A feeling of foreboding gripped her as she turned and pulled off Danny's shoes and helped him into his nightshirt. He placed his arms around her neck and planted a damp kiss on her cheek.

"Momma," he whispered drowsily, "let me say my prayers now. I gotta ask God to help me get big fast."

"But why, Danny? You can't hurry—"

"So I can carry the water for you and earn money, too."

"What of Uncle Willie? That's his job!"

Danny yawned again, "Wil-l-lie." Then his eyelids drooped and with a little sigh, he dropped off to sleep.

CHAPTER 4

Cold rain blew in as November winds howled. The rain in the streets turned to ice, two inches thick, and everything glittered and sparkled when the sun burst through. The brown buffalo grass, already cropped short from overgrazing, looked like slivers of glass. News came that cattle were in danger and some were dying. Few were selling in late autumn, but enough had sold to ease the glut in the cattle market.

Barbara shivered in the big drafty kitchen, and she longed for the cozy warmth of their soddy in the West. She stoked the fire and shook the grate almost constantly to coax more warmth from the old stove. Willie brought in several armloads of wood and piled them in the lean-to each day.

She dressed the boys in extra shirts and trousers to keep them warm. She knew Willie's work outdoors at the lumberyard gave him little time to keep himself warm. He finally bought a pair of gray felt boots which he would pull over the calfskins to keep his feet warm. Then he would put on the undervest Barbara had stitched together from an old flannel blanket. He wore a pair of mittens and a red wool cap she had knitted for him, too. It was during their years at Cottonwood Crossing that she had struggled with knitting needles and finally learned how to knit.

"Here. Let me tie this muffler over your cap," she said,

tucking the fringes under his chin.

"What're ya tryin' to do, Barbara—smother me?" he muttered. "If you bundle me up much more, I can't work! And what about Charlie? Do ya deck him out this way, too?"

She laughed. "The coat he bought at Beebe's is fleece-lined. It has a sort of cover over his head. I made him buy boots with the money you gave us."

"What of the little fellers? They keepin' warm?"

She sighed and pulled the short brown jacket closer around her neck. "Oh, I smother them with extra layers of clothes, and herd them close to the fire. If only this house wasn't so drafty."

"Well, it sure ain't as comfortable as the soddy, that's fer sure," Willie said. "Tell ya what." His voice sounded muffled behind the scarf tied over his face. "Maybe I can bring home extra scraps of lumber and nail them on the walls. It'll help trap some of the warm air in and keep the cold wind out."

He slapped his hands together and stomped out the door. Barbara watched him go. *He's barely 19 and he has to take on a man's job,* she told herself. *What would we ever do without him?*

The wind whistled through the gaps around the windows, and for the next half hour Barbara stuffed rags into the cracks to block the drafts. She was glad the boys were still sleeping, grateful for the warmth under the thick wool comforts and blankets she had tucked over the trundle bed. The ceiling helped trap some of the heat downstairs, but she knew it was bitterly cold on the second floor. The chimney that passed through the south upstairs bedroom ceiling made a feeble attempt to take out some of the chill before it poked through the roof.

She had just settled into a chair beside the fire with some mending when Jem's cry startled her. She laid down Charlie's red plaid flannel shirt and went into the bedroom. The window panes were glazed with opaque ice and she paused to scratch it away on the north window to peek outside. The wind screamed under the eaves. She picked up a folded blanket from the double bed and wrapped it around Jem and carried him into the kitchen.

"I'll get you dressed and give you a hot breakfast," she said. He burrowed his face against her shoulder and grunted like a little pig. "I can't believe you're past two years old, Jem!"

"Me two old," he mumbled, looking anxiously into Barbara's face as she pulled on his warm shirt. "Jem play outside?"

"No, honey. It's very cold out there." She carried him with one arm as she warmed a panful of milk and crumbled a piece of cornbread into a bowl. Then she set him into his high chair.

"I'm glad you're learning to feed yourself. Wasn't it good of Uncle Willie to make this chair for you?"

"Me eat!" He banged his spoon on the edge of the tray-table.

"Let's pray first."

In minutes he had shoveled the breakfast into his mouth while Barbara tossed his night clothes onto a pile of dirty laundry that waited to be washed. She hated to string wet clothes indoors, but there was no other way to dry them with the inclement weather outside.

The wind still pounded and blew against the house, tossing half-frozen fistfuls of rain against the gaunt frame house.

Just then she thought she heard a frantic knocking. Or was it Danny pounding on the bedroom wall? She listened again and opened the outside door cautiously. And icy blast whirled through the crack as she peered out. Then she opened it wider and pulled a bedraggled, wet figure into the kitchen.

"Nance! What in the world are you doing out in this nasty weather? Why didn't you stay in where it's warm?"

Nance Drubeck staggered to a chair and sank into a shivering heap. Her red shawl was encrusted with ice particles, and the thin, threadbare jacket underneath was damp and splotched with mud. Her bare hands were red and cold and her face looked like a puckered, frosted apple. She dropped a shabby valise to the floor.

Straightening suddenly, her green eyes hardened. "I . . . I thought I'd come out and . . . and see you, bein' you said I should."

"Yes, but why venture out in this awful weather? Couldn't you have waited for a nicer day?" Barbara asked, drawing off the wet shawl and rubbing the icy fingers. "You'll catch your death of cold. I don't understand—"

"I got booted out," Nance said bluntly, "if you must know."

"But why? And who'd be so heartless as to throw out someone in this kind of weather?"

Nance rose slowly to her feet and patted her abdomen. "That's why. I'm gonna have a kid in three months. I couldn't hide it no longer. My corsets wouldn't pull in my belly 'cause the stays was hurtin' me, so my boss . . . well, he said I had to go."

Barbara stared at Nance in amazement. "A baby? But Nance —you're not married!"

"Who says you gotta be married to have a baby? Anyhow, the kid's father wouldn't have me anymore, even when I said I'd marry him. I didn't know where to go, so I came here. You said to come."

Drawing a deep breath, Barbara eased Nance back into her chair. What should she do with this . . . "woman of the night" here in her home?

"You just stay here and get warmed up," she said finally. "I'll fix you a hot breakfast and get you into some dry clothes. Maybe one of my dresses—"

"Yeah? How'm I s'posed to squeeze into one of yours with my big belly?" Nance asked as she unbuttoned her shirt.

Barbara helped to pull the soaked, red taffeta over Nance's bedraggled brown hair and tossed it on the floor. She went to the bedroom and came back with one of Charlie's flannel shirts and an old full skirt.

"Here. This is warm and dry. Finish getting out of your wet things. Look at your boots—wet clear through!"

Nance jerked away her arms. "I don't wanna wear a man's shirt! I'm used to wearin' lady stuff!"

Barbara shook her head. "Well, Nance, you can't be choosy, I'm afraid. Besides, I'm not sure what we'll do with you. I have my hands full taking care of my family."

"Humph! I figured you was too goody-goody to take me in. You Christians is all the same. Talk-talk. But you don't mean a word about carin'.'"

"I—" Barbara winced. It was true. She had said she wanted to help Nance, if she was in trouble, but now she found herself resisting. *If I weren't always so infernally tired,* she told herself.

"Nance, I should really discuss this with Charlie and Willie. Perhaps if you could help me while you stay here." She paused and swallowed. "You see, I'm expecting a baby in March, some four months from now, and I get very tired." She picked Jem from his chair and washed his face, and set him in the corner with his toys.

"You can make a big tower all by yourself, Jem, before Danny gets up," she said. Jem was soon rattling with the blocks and screeching at the top of his lungs.

Danny mumbled sleepily from the bedroom, scowling at some secret disgust, his clothes rumpled and half-buttoned.

"Momma, do I hafta play with Jem again? He always messes up what I want to build!"

"Let me button your shirt right and give you some breakfast. And look who's here, Danny. This is . . . Nance. She's going to stay with us for awhile. Maybe she can tell you stories and . . . and things."

Danny stood in front of Nance with his hands behind his back. "You tell me stories about the big bad men who go into the s'loons?"

Nance drew a quick breath, and her green eyes narrowed. "You don't wanna hear stories about those . . . those monsters!" she spat out. "Maybe . . . maybe I'll think of some other story after a bit."

Barbara moved to the stove, stirred the gruel and poured milk into two glasses. "Now you two sit down and eat breakfast. Nance will wash the dishes after you've finished."

Nance gave Barbara a sharp glance. "Look, I ain't said I'd help! It ain't my line of work."

"We don't offer your 'line of work' here, Nance!" Barbara

flared. "I must wash clothes this morning. If you want to stay here and help me, I'll be glad to keep you until . . . until the baby is born. After that, we'll see. Maybe you can get a job as waitress in one of the eating places."

Nance ate hungrily, and Barbara noticed she picked up the dishes and began to wash them after she and Danny had cleaned out their bowls.

Barbara was exhausted when she finished the washing and had hung the clothes on rope lines stretched across the large kitchen. The room had become steamy with dampness, and the windows had fogged up quickly, making the room even darker and more dreary than before. Barbara stepped out to the lean-to and cut a chunk of side beef that hung from the rafters. With Charlie's working on the ranch, he was able to bring home a sizable chunk of meat now and then.

Nance had been silent and morose most of the day, but she grudgingly helped fold the clothes as they dried.

Finally the long day wheeled slowly to a close. The wind and rain had died down and the wan light of the setting sun crept weakly over the horizon. The aroma of bubbling beef in the gray kettle added a soothing atmosphere in the kitchen, although Barbara didn't feel very "soothed" with Nance pouting in one corner.

What'll I tell Charlie and Willie? Barbara wondered as she chopped turnips and carrots, then diced onions for the soup. *And where would Nance sleep?*

Minutes later Willie burst through the door, snatched up the water pails and headed for the town pump. He apparently hadn't noticed Nance, for which Barbara was glad. It gave her more time to formulate an explanation for the girl's presence.

"You think your menfolks'll let me stay? Or will they boot me out, too?" Nance mumbled as she came and leaned over one end of the table.

"No," Barbara said with a patient sigh. "No one will boot you out, Nance. But they will need a logical explanation of why you're here," she said, dumping the vegetables into the simmering beef broth.

Nance frowned. "I . . . I just didn't know where to go, Barbara. And you said if I was in trouble—"

"You said you didn't need anyone, so this was a real surprise. But I really want to help you somehow. What of the child's father?"

The hard look crept into her green eyes again. "A soldier from Fort Harker. I was all 'peaches and cream' until I told him we were gonna have this baby and what was he gonna do about it? He never showed his face again. So I tried to keep away from men after that, but that's not what you do in my line of work. When Hunt Walker, my boss, seen what was happenin', he threw me out. Said he couldn't afford to keep me if I wasn't gonna do the job I was hired to do."

"Where are your things, Nance? Surely you have more belongings."

She pointed to the valise. "This is all I brought. I better not show my face there again, Hunt said. But I forgot my comb and curl-papers and rouge and stuff."

She awkwardly set the flatware on the table as Willie came in with the two pails. He glanced at her sharply, with a question in his eyes.

"This is Nance Drubeck, Willie," Barbara explained quickly. "She's Mame Probst's niece. She'll stay with us for awhile."

He nodded and immediately went to the two small boys who were chattering in one corner.

"Hey, fellers," he said, tousling Jem's hair, "it's Uncle Willie-time!"

Barbara left the stove and looked at him. "Could you please go down to Drover's Cottage and pick up the rest of Nance's things? She didn't bring a comb and other things with her."

He looked at her and started for the door. "Sorry, fellers. I'll be back quick."

Just then Charlie came home with the same questions in his summer blue eyes. Barbara placed a finger to her lips and continued with the cooking until she could step away from the kitchen for a moment to explain Nance's predicament to him.

Two hours later, when the meal was over and the kitchen set to rights, Barbara put the boys to bed. When she returned to the kitchen, she began speaking to the small group that had assembled near the stove. "Since Nance will be staying here, we'll have to decide where she's to sleep. We have the two rooms upstairs, and Willie's room in the south room is warmer. I don't quite know—"

"I'll pile down blankets on the floor of the north room and let her have my bed," Willie offered promptly, "until I rustle me up a bed."

"But that room is cold, Willie," Charlie began. "You work outdoors most of the day."

Nance was seated at one end of the table, her face sullen, and, at Charlie's words, she glanced up sharply.

"Guess I could go out to the shed," she mumbled in a martyr's voice. "No one cares what happens to me anyway."

"No, that isn't so, Nance," Charlie said firmly. "We'll work something out, like Willie said. But the Lord wants you here for now. Please, go on upstairs to the south room. Willie will carry your valise up for you."

After they had left the room, Charlie leaned over and kissed Barbara's cheek. "I don't know about all this," he said quietly. "I only hope this won't be too much for you."

"I already told her she'd have to help," Barbara said with a quiet sigh. "At first she protested that it wasn't in her 'line of work', but I hope I've convinced her she'd have to do her part if she stays here. She has pitched in a little, although she won't talk much."

"Let's go to bed, my darling," Charlie said, helping her to her feet. "You're so tired right now that you're ready to drop. I only hope all this won't be too hard on you," he said again. "Maybe with God's help . . ."

She sighed as she pulled off the faded percale and drew on her long flannel nightgown, then sat down to braid her hair.

"As you said, the Lord will give grace. Just maybe I can help her and make a difference in her life."

He tucked the covers around her and drew her into his

arms. "If anyone can help her, Barbara, you can. Just don't try too hard, and wear yourself out."

She leaned against his chest. *Oh, dear Lord,* she prayed, *this won't be easy, but what else can I do?*

CHAPTER 5

*I*n the morning the sun shone cold and brittle. The ice had made the road past the house raw and muddy, and everything lay sodden under the cold, heavy air.

Willie stomped in at noon, carrying a small Lady Franklin stove which he promptly lugged upstairs and set up. His face, sooty and covered with sweat when he came downstairs, was creased into a grin.

"It was settin' in a shed behind the lumberyard and they said I could take it if I wanted to clean it up. Now we can keep a fire in Nance's room," he said sitting down to eat Barbara's beef stew. If Nance appreciated the gesture, she said nothing.

She was sullen and uncommunicative and made only a few feeble efforts to help with the work. Now and then Nance, ungainly in Charlie's big shirt and Barbara's coarse brown skirt, cleared away the dishes.

As Willie finished the last of his stew, he bundled into his warm wraps. Before he left, he paused for a rousing romp with the "fellers," which left them ready for a nap.

"I'm to help take out a load of lumber some ten miles west this afternoon," he said as he started for the door. "I might be a bit late comin' home this evenin', since I'm to ride out to the Comstock spread with a keg of nails afterwards for the barn they're buildin'. It'll take most of the rest of the day."

Barbara gave his arm a gentle squeeze. "As long as you get back in time to fill the water pails! I know Charlie will be tired when he comes in tonight."

"My brother's workin' much too hard," Willie said, "but you can't tell him that. He's so set on makin' good."

"I know, and I love him for his determination. It's not like it used to be when he always came for dinner. But I know he gets a hearty meal at the mess hall on the ranch, and I'm grateful for that. But when both you and Charlie are gone all day, I feel so alone!"

Willie nodded in Nance's direction. "Is she helpin' chase some of the lonesomeness?" His voice was low.

Barbara sighed. "Not much. But it's good having someone around besides the boys. I only hope I can do something to help her." She shrugged her shoulders.

He left then, and she went back to the table to clear away the food.

Nance was standing at the east window and gazed after Willie. "You had him with you long?"

"Willie? He's always been a part of the family. When Charlie's and Willie's parents and their sister, Nellie May, were killed by Indians on their way to Kansas some 10 years ago, Charlie took over the care of his only brother."

"You don't mind his livin' with you?"

"Why should I? Actually, Willie was the first real friend I made in Kansas. And we're still friends. I trust him as much as I trust Charlie."

Nance drummed her fingers on the window sill. "He sure seems taken up with your young'uns."

"Yes, he's always done so, ever since they were born."

Barbara wiped the table and set the sad irons on the stove. The ironing job would take most of the day. She was glad the boys were napping, and she opened the bedroom door so the room would remain warm.

Rolling out one dampened garment on the mat she had placed on the table, she said, "It was thoughtful of Willie to bring in the stove for your room, wasn't it?"

"It'll help to keep me warm at night—bein's I don't have no man in bed with me," she bit out a sarcastic reply. "If that's what you was drivin' at."

Barbara chewed on her lip. "No, I didn't meant that! But that's how Willie is—always thoughtful and courteous."

"Didn't ever have nobody I could trust," Nance said sullenly. "But everyone has a shifty reason for what they do. Wonder what his was?"

"There's no shifty reason at all." Barbara snapped. "Did it ever occur to you there are people in this world who don't need an ulterior motive to do good?" She shook out Charlie's Sunday shirt and hung it over the back of the chair.

"Not in this town, there aren't. So don't snap at me," Nance growled. "In my life, all I've seen is dog-eat-dog. I only hope you're right . . . about Willie." She moved away from the window, drew a comb from her pocket and began to comb the tangles from her long, brown hair.

As Barbara watched Nance untangle her drab brown tresses, her thoughts drifted to the Moores. *Dear Aunt Prudy and Uncle Daniel Moore . . . and my dear cousins to whom I'll be eternally grateful for teaching me the necessities of prairie life and much, much more. Their jovial ways, their constant chatter!*

Cousin Aggie had compared Cousin Bitsy's golden tresses to "egg yolk—not gold" during their banter of teasing and joking when they were all together back at the Moores' cabin near Council Grove. How Barbara missed her Moore cousins!

With fond memories she recalled them one by one: Aggie was the second oldest to Cousin Rosie, who was married to John Frazer. Rosie taught Barbara the virtue of patience with her trust in the Lord during the tragic illness of her baby.

Cousin Josh was next in line after Aggie. Josh had lost a leg in the Civil War, but he'd never allowed it to make him bitter.

Vange, beautiful Evangeline, who was married to Barry Keaton in 1865, now lived in Denver, where Barry worked for a newspaper.

The youngest Moore, Elisabeth, always known as Bitsy,

married Merritt Wallace the winter after they met on the trip home from Atlanta. They were living in Manhattan, Kansas, where Merritt was a professor at Bluemont College. By now the Wallaces had two children.

Barbara knew she'd never forget her lively cousins who found the funny side to every situation. *I don't know how I would've survived without their sense of humor,* she mused, *even though I didn't like it when I first moved in with them.* She remembered how Aunt Prudy mercifully "shushed" the girls when their laughter became too boisterous for Barbara or the rest of the household. Barbara knew she'd be forever in debt to Uncle Daniel and his precious family, for had it not been for their love and care and their strong faith in God, she'd never have made it.

"God bless them all!" she whispered under her breath.

"What'd you say?" Nance looked at her with a startled expression.

"Oh, nothing. I was just talking to myself."

The afternoon waned, and Barbara had just put away the last of the ironing when she glanced at the Seth Thomas clock. It was almost time for Willie to come home. The beans had simmered with a chunk of salt pork in the pot on the back burner for hours, and it was time to put the turnips on to boil.

The boys had been playing quietly for some time, and Barbara gave them a mail order catalog to look at. They exclaimed at all the unusual items and wanted to know what they were for.

As the hour dragged on and Willie hadn't come, she felt a vague uneasiness.

"Wonder where Willie is," she said aloud, moving the beans back to the rear of the stove.

"He said he'd be late, didn't he?" Nance muttered, standing at the window again.

"Yes, that's what he said."

Already dusk had fallen and the afterglow deepened from soft rose to purple as misty lavender filled the lengthening shadows in the trailing twilight.

"Where's Unca Willie?" Jem fretted, clinging to Barbara's skirt.

"He said he'd be late today, Honey. Just be patient. He'll be here soon."

The water pails were empty and Barbara needed to fix coffee. Just then Charlie rode in. When he slammed into the kitchen, she grabbed the pails and handed them to him.

"Would you mind? Willie hasn't come home and we're out."

"What's keeping him? He's usually home an hour before I get here."

"He said he was to help deliver some lumber west of town and warned it could get late."

As Charlie left the house, Barbara tried to push her worries from her mind. Surely Willie would breeze in any minute. She washed the boys, then spooned the beans into bowls.

Their evening meal, when Charlie came back, was silent. Willie's absence hung over the kitchen like a heavy curtain.

"He could still come, even if it's late." Barbara said in a low voice. "He did say he might be late, after delivering the nails. But it's long dark—"

Charlie got up from the table and pulled on his jacket. "I'll go down to the lumberyard to see if anyone knows anything," he said, and slammed out the door.

"I've been praying that Willie will be fine wherever he is," Barbara said as she shoved the boys into the bedroom. They had clamored for Uncle Willie's good-night romp as usual.

"You don't expect God to have all the answers?" Nance snapped, pulling off her boots and wiggling her dainty feet.

"The Lord will send His angels to take charge over Willie. The Bible assures us of this," Barbara called over her shoulder. "The Bible also says that God's ways aren't always our ways. Maybe He has the answer to Willie's lateness. We must accept His will, although I firmly believe he will be all right and come home soon."

Just then Charlie came into the kitchen with a blast of cold air. *Had he already been to see Willie's boss?* she wondered.

The grim look on his face startled Barbara. "Charlie? What . . . where is Willie?"

Charlie shrugged out of his jacket and took Barbara's shoulders between his hands. "They . . . they don't know. He and one of the other employees took the load of lumber to the Richards all right, the man said. Then Willie was to ride out to the Comstocks with the nails. He . . . he never came back. They don't know what's happened or where he is. He's probably been delayed there and will return in the morning. Let's leave it in God's hands and trust him to come back safely."

"If you ask me," Nance grunted, "he took off while he had the chance. Any boy who works hard to help his family, totes all them buckets of water, and is expected to turn over his earnin's can be expected to skip out the first chance he gets. He's just mad that he had to give up his room."

"Willie's not like that!" Barbara spat out. "He'll be back in the morning. Just wait and see."

She made her way wearily into the bedroom, the feeling of foreboding gripping her heart in spite of her brave words of assurance.

Oh dear God, be with Willie, wherever he is! Please let him be all right.

CHAPTER 6

$\mathcal{B}$arbara tossed restlessly through the night. With every creak of the rafters she sat upright, listening for Willie's footsteps, praying over and over for his safety. The yellow cowslip moon swung out into the night sky, cold and brittle as the stars that hung in the black heavens. Somewhere in the distance, the howl of a coyote awakened her from her light dozing, while a mourning dove cooed to its mate outside the bedroom window. The Seth Thomas clock ticked ponderously on its shelf in the kitchen, echoing loudly in the silent house.

Jem stirred with a little whimper, and several times Barbara slipped out of bed to tuck the warm covers around him.

"Barbara?" Charlie called softly. "You up?"

She came back to the warm cocoon of their bed covers. "I couldn't sleep, so I checked on the boys."

"I guess Willie hasn't come in yet?"

"No. I'd have heard him."

He gently placed an arm around her shoulders. "Please leave Willie in the Lord's hands. There's nothing we can do."

"I know. But I worry anyhow. If he isn't home by morning, Charlie, what shall we do?" she asked in a voice thick with anxiety. "I've prayed and prayed, but there's no peace!"

"If I didn't have to ride out to the ranch so early, I'd talk to the sheriff. Maybe he'll know something, although the law's pretty well under the thumb of the city fathers, it seems."

"But aren't the lawmen supposed to be aware of any shenanigans?" she asked. "I must believe there'll be an answer by morning."

"Perhaps, my darling. But you need the rest. Let's pray once more."

Charlie drew her close and asked God again to take care of Willie and to bring him home safely.

"And help that our faith won't be shaken in all this," Barbara added. Then she closed her eyes and willed them to sleep.

She awoke later than usual as bright, morning sunlight stabbed through the cold windows. She got up and dressed hurriedly. Charlie had already built a fire in the kitchen range.

"I'd better haul in more fuel for you," he said, tugging on his heavy coat. "Meanwhile, keep up your courage. We're bound to have some news before long. Remember—God's in control. We must believe that."

After Charlie had left for work, Barbara got the boys up and gave them breakfast, one eye on the outside door, expecting Willie to burst in at any moment.

When Nance dragged herself down the stairs an hour later, she rubbed her eyes and yawned.

"Willie come in yet?" she mumbled.

"Not yet. I'm plenty worried, Nance. I can't see any good reason why he shouldn't have come home."

"You won't believe he just decided to walk out, will you?" The sullen words were gritty. "He skipped out while the goin' was good. Mark my words."

Barbara stoked the fire. "I'll never believe that! I've been praying all morning. Surely the Lord—"

"What for? As if God cares about anyone in this God-for-saken country! I say, you're wastin' your breath, expectin' some sort of miracle."

Jem fussed and fretted again, and she grew distraught in trying to calm him on top of everything else.

Danny tugged impatiently at her skirt. "I guess Uncle Willie went to work early. He didn't tell us goodbye," he pouted. "I wish he was home!"

"So do I," Barbara said softly. "Let's keep on asking Jesus to watch over him and bless him while he's on his way, just as He takes care of all His sheep that are in His care."

"You don't actually teach your young'uns all that stuff about God's love, do ya?" Nance scoffed. "Why don't you do somethin', instead of beggin' your God to do it all for ya?"

Barbara was driven into silence. What had Charlie said? If he hadn't had to leave for work so early, he'd have talked to the sheriff.

Suddenly she glanced at Nance. The girl stared back with a dull look in her jade-green eyes.

"Nance, you've given me an idea. Would you look after the boys for about an hour? I'll hurry to the sheriff's office and see what I can learn. I'll make sure the fire's all right. Would you do it for me, please?"

Nance stared at her lap that was fast disappearing into a balloon. "Guess so. As long as you keep me until my kid's born. Could you stop by the drugstore and bring me some sleepin' potions? I ain't been sleepin' so good."

"Yes, I'll do that. Just make sure the boys don't get too rowdy. And above all, don't let them go outside. It's too cold for that."

As she was speaking she bundled herself into her shabby brown coat and jammed the red wool cap onto her head. She checked the fire, then tied her muffler under her chin, kissed the boys, and started for the door.

"Momma will be back soon," she said briskly. "Nance will look after you. I know you'll be good boys. Danny, help her with Jem if you can."

Danny stretched himself as tall as possible. "Sure, I'm a big boy, and if Uncle Willie stays gone long I'll get a job."

As Barbara stepped outside, his words lingered in her ears. A job? If Willie's absence dragged out, they'd need more income. How would they ever manage?

The streets were empty except for a few wagons and buggies that clattered toward the business section. As she pushed herself the two blocks toward the main part of town, a sharp wind gusted down the main thoroughfare with a rattle of dry leaves and crumpled paper. *The sheriff's office must be near the courthouse,* she reasoned.

As she crossed the plaza and the tracks from the south, she saw it next to the *Reporter* office. In her hurry to get to the sheriff, she tripped over the rough boards and caught herself just before she fell. *I must watch out,* she told herself. *We have enough trouble.*

The courthouse, built of bricks, was a heavy two-story structure. She opened the big front door and stepped inside. Sheriff Kingsley was hunched over his desk, his salt-and-pepper head with its handlebar mustache bent over a stack of papers. He took his pipe from his mouth and stared at her.

Barbara walked hesitantly toward his desk and paused.

"Yes?" he stopped to knock the dottle from his pipe. "What can I do for you?"

"I . . . I'm Barbara Warren. We . . . my husband Charlie and I moved to Ellsworth last September with our two sons and Charlie's brother Willie. Charlie's working on the Wilcox Ranch and Willie has a job at the lumberyard. But last night, Willie didn't come home. He's still not back and we're worried."

Sheriff lit his pipe again. "Well, this is only the next mornin' after last night, so why are you worried?"

"Because we don't know what's happened to him! He's only 18. Yesterday he helped unload some lumber on the Richards' place. Then he was to ride out to the Comstocks with a keg of nails. He . . . he hasn't returned."

Amusement glinted in the sheriff's pale gray eyes. "Look, lady, if you're worried about a little thing like that—"

"It's not a little thing!" she flared. She was growing agitated from the whole ordeal. "A person's missing. Isn't it a sheriff's job to check this out?"

He tapped his pipe on the edge of the desk and eyed her shrewdly. "It don't make sense. Young boys come and go. He's off on some lark, if you ask me."

"But Willie's not like that. He'd never go off unless he told us!"

"Forget it, Lady. Tell him to come see me when he gits back." He grinned as a puff of smoke curled out from the corners of his mouth. "You just bet your boots he'll be back by nightfall."

Wearily, Barbara thanked him and started for the door. The sheriff seemed totally unconcerned. *How could he be so callous? If only more townspeople cared,* she thought. *Especially someone who should have a reputation for honesty and dedication to his job.*

With a sigh she headed west for Seitz Drugstore. She wasn't too eager to fill Nance's request for the laudanum, but she had promised she would so Nance would stay with the boys.

The funny little man with a bald spot on his head and wearing bifocals left his pestle and bobbed from behind the counter with a polite bow. The small shop reeked with a mixture of spirits and sulphur, and Barbara almost gagged on the odors.

"McClellan Dobbs at your service, ma'am. And what may I do for you?"

"It . . . it's not for myself, but my . . . my friend. Nance Drubeck asked me to drop by for some laudanum. She has had trouble sleeping, she says."

"No doubt!" An amused look glimmered in his small brown eyes. "She hasn't paid her last bill, you know. Do you know—?"

"She's left her previous place of . . . of employment," Barbara stammered, "and is staying with us. I'm Barbara Warren. Perhaps—"

"You're Mrs. Warren?" the man said. "I'm Mr. Seitz's employee. I believe I spoke to a young fella named Willie Warren some days back, about you bein' interested in givin' me room and board. I'm a bachelor, a church man, and I don't hanker staying in them brothels . . . er . . . I mean, boarding houses. I'd prefer a decent place. If you could give me a room and my meals, I'll pay what's fair, and even help around the place. I'd be mighty obliged if you'd do so."

A sudden lilt nudged Barbara's spine. "Oh, would you?

You're a real answer to my prayers. You see, Willie . . ." In a few minutes she had told him about Willie's disappearance.

He wrapped the small vial of laudanum in a piece of brown paper and handed it to Barbara. "Tell Miss Drubeck to go easy on this stuff. It can be very potent. I'll see you after work tonight."

Grabbing her purchase, Barbara left the drugstore and hurried down the street toward their shabby two-story house. At least, this would provide some income as long as Willie wasn't home. *But Lord,* she prayed, *You'll bring him home soon, won't You?*

When she walked in the door the boys were busily hanging a paper chain Nance had made from newspaper strips she had glued together.

"Look what Nance made for us!" Danny exclaimed. "We're gonna hang them on the walls to make them more purty."

"That's . . . that's nice," Barbara mumbled.

Turning to Nance, she handed her the parcel and gave her the pharmacist's admonition to "go easy on it."

"It looks as though you thought of something for the boys to do."

"Oh, they was belly-achin' about their blocks and I got tired of it. I remembered this is what I done when . . . when my Ma . . . when I was still a decent girl."

"But you're still a decent girl, Nance," Barbara said. "You've just lost your way. Some day—"

"Don't count on it. I'm a whore, and don't you forget it!"

"But you don't have to be this way, Nance. God can always change —"

"You leave God outta this," she snapped. Then she sobered. "What's the sheriff say?"

Barbara sighed. "He thinks we're worrying needlessly. That Willie will come back on his own."

"See? That's what I been tellin' ya. Well, if you get too desperate, you can always ask the soldiers at Fort Harker to search. They'll figure out if it was Indians that took him."

"Indians? But I've been told they're on the reservations now.

Surely they wouldn't—"

"Never trust a Cheyenne Dog Indian. They still roam all over."

Barbara tried to push the thought from her mind. It hadn't occurred to her that Indians might have been in the area. She told Nance about McClellan Dobbs and his search for a place to board.

"He can have the bed Willie built in the other upstairs room . . . until Willie comes back." Barbara said.

"Well, don't count on Willie's comin' back right away," Nance's responded sullenly. "Now I can get Clell Dobbs to bring me my drugs when I need them."

That evening when Charlie rode up, Barbara mentioned Nance's suggestion about talking to the soldiers at the fort. She explained the lack of response from the sheriff.

Charlie shook his head and said, "I checked back at the lumberyard on the way home today and they said the Comstocks got their nails from Willie. So he must've disappeared after that." Charlie ate his meal quickly, then saddled up and headed out toward Fort Harker.

In all the excitement she had forgotten to mention the pharmacist. The little man came in for a late meal shortly after Charlie left, and Barbara dished up a bowl full of stew for him. Barbara paused to bow her head in prayer with him when he gave thanks.

"This is good grub," he said after he had finished. "I'll feel at home here with your family. And a family who prays, too."

Barbara heard Nance's snort behind her and smiled a little. It wouldn't hurt the girl to know there were others who believed in God.

Clell Dobbs took to the boys immediately, and they soon romped on the floor until she announced their bedtime.

The little druggist had gone upstairs. Nance sat plaiting her long brown hair into braids and then went up to her bed.

Barbara got the boys ready for night just before Charlie came in.

"They'll send out a search party in the morning," he said.

"All we can do now is wait—and trust some more."

Just then Clell Dobbs came downstairs. "Oh, I'm Clell—" he began with embarrassment.

"Charlie, this is McClellan Dobbs. He works at the Seitz Drugstore, and asked for a room and meals. It will help us out—until Willie comes back."

Charlie shook hands with the strong, thin fingers. "Welcome, Clell. As you see, you've caught us in something of a turmoil, since my brother seems to be missing."

"That's quite all right. As I told Mrs. Warren, I wanted to stay in a private home and I'm thankful to have found yours. I'll remember you in my prayers." He paused for a drink of water, picked up an armload of wood and crept back up the stairs.

"I just hope this won't give you more work than necessary," Charlie said slowly. "You're always so tired."

"But Mr. Dobbs has promised to help. He'll carry water and bring in stove wood."

"That'll help. But promise me you won't overdo."

As the next few days went by, Barbara's prayers for Willie's return continued. Each day she watched the door anxiously, waiting for Willie or for a soldier to stop by with word of his wherabouts.

"I sure don't look forward to seein' any soldiers," Nance sputtered when Barbara told her they were searching. "They ain't up to no good. Let me know when they come so I can hide."

"But why hide, Nance? If they bring good news, or any kind of news—"

"Don't forget, they was some of my best . . . er . . . customers. Especially one handsome scalawag! I don't want to see him. He's responsible for . . . this." She patted her abdomen again.

"You don't have to see him, Nance," Barbara said. "All we want is word about Willie. I'll answer any knock on the door."

But as the days went by and there was no word, Barbara stepped up her prayers. *Dear Lord,* she prayed, *I've trusted You with my life many times; now I'm asking You to help me trust You with Willie's.*

Nance seemed more tired than usual and kept to herself in her room most of the day. Barbara sighed. The girl was without her usual snap and crackle. The baby's birth was still two months away. *I'll be glad when the ordeal is over,* Barbara thought.

Just then a frantic knock sounded on the door, and Barbara hurried to open it. There stood a soldier, his blue cap in his hands.

"Ma'am? Miz Warren? We been searchin' the area 10 to 20 miles west. We found no sign of the young man. All we picked up was this —" He reached into his pocket and drew out a red wool knitted cap.

"That's Willie's!" she cried, grabbing it away from him. "He wore it the day he disappeared. Was there . . . anything else? A sign of a skirmish, any hoof tracks . . . anything?"

"No ma'am. As I said, this was all. We're surmisin' maybe he was s'prised by Injuns. The ranchers around there say they seen a few Cheyenne bucks lopin' down the Smoky Hill Trail some days ago, but that was all. We done all we could do. No sign of him."

A dull pain wrenched through Barbara at his words. *Was Willie lost from them forever?* She refused to believe it.

"Th . . . thank you, sir. Thank you for your trouble."

"No trouble, ma'am. It's our job."

She made her way slowly to the bedroom after he left and threw herself on the bed, clutching Willie's cap to her breast. Her heart suddenly felt very heavy.

"Dear God," she cried. "This can't be the answer! I won't accept it as final!"

After her tears had spent themselves, she got up, washed her face and began to prepare supper, almost in a trance. *It wasn't true—it couldn't be true! Willie would come back.* She felt almost the same as the time when she had received word that Matthew Potter had died. Then it had been true.

I must hang onto my sanity, she told herself. *Charlie—the boys, Nance and Clell Dobbs need me. I must be strong. God, help me to hang on!*

December came with cold winds and pale winter sunlight. The world spun on its way as though nothing had changed. Barbara felt numb as she prepared meals and took care of the house. True to his promise, Clell Dobbs carried in wood and brought water. The boys seemed to adore him.

Nance showed little interest in anything these days. She spent most of her time in the large south bedroom upstairs, reading a few cheap romance novels, while she helped Barbara less than ever.

One day when the sharp winds gusted under the eaves, she came downstairs, clutching her abdomen.

"Barb'ra . . . I . . . I think it's time—"

"Time? But not for another month or so, you said. Are you sure?" Barbara gasped, alarmed at the stricken look on Nance's face.

But without another word she led the girl to the downstairs bed and pulled back the covers. "You . . . just lie back. I . . . I'll have to bundle up Danny and send him for the doctor. Just try to relax."

Explaining to Danny where to go, she dressed him warmly, praying all the while. "Tell the doctor to hurry. We need him very bad!" Then she led him to the door and watched him trundle down the cold, windswept street.

She tried to make Nance comfortable, but the girl wailed and screamed. Jem grew upset, and began to shriek in terror.

"Momma . . . Momma . . . I hurt, too!"

After she set a kettle of water to boil on the stove, she picked him up and held him against her, stroking his tossled hair while waiting at the door for Dr. Henson's arrival. She carried the water to the nightstand at Nance's bedside.

When he came with Danny, she ushered him immediately to the bedroom. He looked competent and set to work, opening his black bag for his necessary equipment.

"I'll need more hot water," he ordered briskly.

She sat Jem in the corner with Danny and the wooden blocks and poured the last of the water from the pail into another kettle on the stove.

Nance's screams and wails continued. Barbara sat beside the bed and took her carefully manicured hand in her own rough one and rubbed it gently.

The doctor worked quietly and efficiently. Then after Nance's long, last wail, he snatched up a scrap of old blanket, and turned to Barbara with a tired sigh.

"It's a girl. I'm sorry . . . but the baby is dead."

Barbara drew a ragged breath. She looked at the wrinkled newborn. It was beautiful and looked as fragile as a porcelain doll. It couldn't be dead! Wordlessly she stroked Nance's damp face.

"Nance," she whispered, "It's . . . a girl. A beautiful little doll. But . . . I'm so sorry. It . . . Here, let me show you."

Barbara took the baby with the blanket wrapped around its lifeless form. A look of comprehension dawned on Nance's face, and she shook her head fiercely. "No! I don't want to see it. Just leave me alone!" She closed her eyes and tried to roll on her side away from Barbara.

The doctor handed Barbara a small vial. "Here's something to calm her down, if she needs it. She's obviously very upset. You take care of this . . . this infant."

Horror-struck, Barbara carried the stillborn child to the kitchen while the doctor let himself out. *Dear God,* she prayed, *what shall I do with it?*

CHAPTER 7

$\mathcal{B}$arbara was scarcely aware that Clell Dobbs had come in. He took one look at the situation and left. Barbara sat holding Nance's lifeless baby in her arms as a wave of despair swept over her. *Oh, dear God, what next?* she moaned. She closed her eyes to blot out everything around her.

Twenty minutes later Clell was back, bringing Pastor Levi Sternberg with him. "Here's the parson, ma'am," he said. "He'll handle things. I'll fix up a box for the buryin'. If you can spare a little baby dress—"

"Oh, yes." Barbara's voice was breathless. She was grateful to have someone to share this unforeseen burden with her. She laid the blanketed infant in Pastor Sternberg's arms and went into the bedroom to search among her box of baby clothes.

Nance had turned her face to the wall and refused to look up. Pawing through the tiny garments, Barbara found a little dress trimmed in blue embroidery. Her Cousin Aggie had made it for Jem when he was an infant. She flung it over her arm and hurried back into the kitchen. The pastor sat on the good chair, still holding the dead child.

"We'll lay it out in the box Brother Dobbs is nailing together, and I'll say a brief service over it," he said softly. "How is the mother taking it?"

Barbara drew her breath sharply. "She . . . she says she doesn't want to see it. To her it was just a . . . a," she paused, groping for the right words.

"Brother Dobbs said it was a 'colt's child,' a bastard child. But the Lord's mercy is great enough to receive even the least of these."

"Yes," Barbara whispered. She stirred the fire until it blazed with warmth; then she added more wood. It was time to prepare the evening meal.

After the pastor left, she began to whip up the inevitable batch of cornbread. Mercifully, the boys played quietly in their corner with their blocks of wood.

When Charlie came home, she told him what had happened, then burst into tears. He took her into his arms and stroked her hair gently. "Oh, my poor darling, you've had so much to bear. If I'd only known! What can I do to help?"

"Just hold me; then take care of the boys," she whispered hoarsely.

"Of course." He kissed her gently, then turned to Danny and Jem. Danny tried to look grown-up, but Jem started fretting and whimpering again. Barbara clapped her hands over her ears and wept.

The next hour dragged. When Clell came in carrying the small pine box, she composed herself. *I can't fail Nance now,* she thought. She snatched up the little white shawl she was knitting for her own expected child and handed it to Clell.

"Here. Please wrap the baby in this."

Pastor Sternberg, who had returned, had already dressed the infant in the long white dress, and in minutes he had gently wrapped it in the shawl and laid it in the fragrant box that Clell had quickly assembled.

Tears stung Barbara's eyes. The child looked more like a porcelain doll than ever.

"I'll let the mother see it, then I'll bury it in the church yard," the pastor said.

Barbara frowned. "Follow me into the bedroom—although I can't promise what Nance's reaction will be."

48

When they walked toward the bed, Barbara laid one hand on Nance's shoulder. "We brought the baby for you to see," she said softly.

Nance flung off Barbara's arm. "Get out!" she shrieked. "I told you I didn't want to see it. Get that thing out of here!" She pulled the covers over her face and turned to the wall again.

"But this is your child, Miss Drubeck. Surely you want to see how precious, how beautiful she is," Pastor Sternberg said gently.

"I said get out!" Nance mumbled from under the covers. "I told you I want nothing to do with it!"

The pastor held the fragrant pine box in one arm and raised his right hand as if in blessing and said, " 'The Lord giveth and the Lord taketh away. Blessed be the name of the Lord.' Miss Drubeck, please be assured of God's love—"

Nance threw back the covers and sat up, her face livid with anger. "Don't you understand? God hasn't done anythin' for me, and I don't need Him now! Please leave me alone!" She turned her stricken face to the wall again.

Without a word Barbara followed the minister out of the room. He shrugged into his great coat, picked up the tiny coffin and started silently toward the door. The he turned to Barbara. "The girl's spirit is crushed. Never fear. I'll say a brief service and commit the body to dust." Without another word, he walked out into the night.

Barbara, weary with grief and her own discomfort, went into Charlie's arms and cried. *How could Nance be so callous, so utterly bitter and hard? Oh, Lord, please accept my grief for the tears Nance refuses to shed.*

Then she turned to her work at the stove once more.

The evening meal was silent, except for Jem's demands for more milk and cornbread. Even Danny was unusually quiet.

Clell began to clear away the dishes and picked up the dish pan. "You're tired, ma'am," he said. "Let me take care of this. Then I'll go after water."

Barbara looked at Charlie. "Nance will need to go up to her

room. Why don't you stir the fire in the little upstairs stove? Maybe we can persuade her to go up to bed."

When Barbara came into the bedroom, Nance had uncovered her face and lay staring at the ceiling. "Is he gone? Did he take it away?" she muttered.

"Yes," Barbara said. "Pastor Sternberg has left. And you'd better go upstairs to bed. We all need a good night of rest."

"I . . . I feel so weak. I don't know if I can climb the stairs."

"Don't worry. Charlie will carry you."

Nance nodded. "I guess I really pulled a nasty trick on you, havin' my kid too early."

"That's something we can't always control. I'm glad Danny was able to go after the doctor. But death happens all too often here on the raw prairies."

"Don't I know it," Nance snorted.

Charlie came back shortly and picked up Nance's slight figure. "Now I'll take you upstairs."

As Charlie and Nance started for the stairs, Barbara went to the boys and drew them away from their play. Clell Dobbs had already left with the water pails.

"It's time you go to bed, too," she said in a tired voice. Jem began to whimper as she drew off his shoes and socks. "Me wanna see the baby!" he wailed.

"But it's dead!" Danny spat out. "Like the time Uncle Willie's Mogie got dead, remember?"

"Oh," Barbara drew in her breath. Willie's dog, which Henry and Mame Probst had given him for Christmas six years ago, had died the summer before, after a steer had kicked her.

"Danny, this was different. This was a baby, and God took her to heaven."

"But I saw her in the box!" Danny said crossly. "It's dead, like Mogie!"

Barbara shook her head helplessly. *How did one explain death to a child?*

"No, Danny. The baby's *body* is dead, but her spirit, the part that was alive once, is with Jesus. Some day when you're older, maybe I can explain so you'll understand. Now it's time for bed."

Charlie had come downstairs and stood listening. Quietly he picked up Jem and carried him into the bedroom, and Barbara followed a bewildered Danny.

"Let me tuck them in," Charlie said. "You get ready for bed, too. You're ready to drop."

"Oh, Charlie! First, Willie's disappearance. And then Nance's premature baby born dead. Then her refusal to see it. I can't see how—"

"Leave her alone for now. She's still feeling miserable. She needs time to heal," Charlie said, helping her out of her dress. It felt good to crawl into bed. She was drowsy, but she heard Charlie tell the boys that God loved them and that they had nothing to fear. She was so tired. *I wish I could sleep for a week,* she thought. *I hardly feel like doing anything . . . But I can't fail my family.*

For the next several days Nance stayed upstairs in her room. Barbara carried up nourishing soups and broths to her, although the girl hardly spoke. Outside the cold wind mourned and wept, rubbing its sad cheek against the icy windowpanes. Barbara felt alone with the wind and the icy drizzle.

One day when Clell came into the kitchen with a blast of cold air, he nodded in the direction of the stairs.

"She's still up there? Hasn't she come down yet?"

"No. I guess she's not up to it."

"It's been a week, hasn't it?"

"Yes." Barbara nodded. "Women usually stay down a week or ten days after giving birth."

"She still shuttin' up about it?"

"You mean, does she ever speak of her baby? Oh, no. And I don't dare mention it, either," Barbara said.

"Maybe it's time she gets up and makes herself useful. She don't expect you to wait on her forever, does she?"

Barbara sighed. "I . . . really don't do much more than take up her meals, and a wash bowl with water for her, and empty her slop jar. But I'm beginning to worry about her. She's becoming more withdrawn than ever."

"Well, she's a queer one. Let me know if I can help."

"Thank you, Clell. You've been very helpful already—carrying water and keeping the wood box filled."

"Parson been here to visit yet?"

Barbara shook her head. "I guess Nance would throw him out, and he knows it."

"I mean, to talk to you. Seems you could do with a bit of comfort yourself."

She smiled wanly. "I have Charlie, except he's so tired when he comes home. We're just drifting along, I guess."

If she could manage to cook the meals, take care of the washing and look after the boys, she would be satisfied. But she was beginning to lose interest in everything. There was still no word from Willie, and Barbara had almost resigned herself to accept God's will. She had prayed and prayed, but there had been no answer.

Clell had seemed to sense her loss of interest and began to entertain the boys when he came from work. He brought empty pill bottles for them to fill with sand, and for awhile this became a favorite pastime.

Once he brought a book of children's stories and took Jem on his knee as he read aloud before supper. Jem was imitating Peter Rabbit as he hopped around the floor. Danny clamored to hold the book, and before long he was pretending to read aloud.

"Look, Momma," he said one day. "I can read all about Peter Rabbit to Jem!"

"But Danny, you're not reading. You're just saying what Clell has read to you."

"If you teach me, I could read, couldn't I?" he asked eagerly.

"If I'd teach you? Well, I helped Willie learn to read," Barbara replied as she paused to ponder the idea. Danny was going to be seven in the spring, and he was old enough to learn the alphabet.

"Well, maybe we can try," she said with a little smile. At least, it would give her a chance to sit down and relax.

Now and then Nance came down for a few minutes, then dragged herself upstairs. Barbara asked if she could come down to eat, but the girl simply shrugged and muttered, "Guess so," then hurried back up to her room.

A few days later Clell Dobbs brought home a stranger. The man he half-carried into the kitchen looked young—not over 25, and he was obviously ill.

"This is Ed Curtis," Clell said by the way of introduction. "Late from Oregon. He needs a place to stay for a few weeks. He can share my bed." Without a word, he struggled to help the man up the stairs.

Barbara watched them go. *Now what in the world was this all about?* she thought. The man was ill, and the whole business puzzled her. *Why did Clell Dobbs bring this stranger without asking me, when he knew how overly tired I am?*

When Clell came downstairs, Danny was laboriously reading the story of Peter Rabbit aloud.

"Looks like you done me out of a job, Danny," he chuckled. "When did you learn to do that?"

"Momma teached me," Danny said proudly. "Now I can read to Jem so Momma can do her work better."

Barbara was at the table, ironing the week's wash. "Yes, and I have plenty to do without more work . . . without the stranger you brought in," she snapped. Before she knew it, she had vented her anger at Clell for the liberty he took by bringing the man.

"Please, ma'am, let me explain. This man came on the noon train. He'd been shot. Injuns paid a surprise visit at the last station. This Ed Curtis is a missionary to the Klamaths out in Oregon. He was on his way home to St. Louis. Well, he was bleedin' bad, so the conductor helped him off and brought him to Doc Henson's office. Henson asked me to come with the proper medicines from the drugstore. Actually, the man was about to die. What do we do with him? He ain't fit to travel. So I said I'd bring him here."

"But you know I have enough to do without adding to my work nursing a sick man!" Barbara exploded. "Taking care of my family and that . . . that girl upstairs—"

"That's the whole point. She's doin' nothin' but rottin' away up there with her cheap novels. So I thought Miz Drubeck could do the nursin'—"

"Nance Drubeck!" Barbara laughed shrilly. "I'd like to see her—"

"Leave her to me," Clell cut in quietly.

Barbara let out a long, drawn-out sigh. She felt sorry for Ed Curtis, but it was almost too much to think of him upstairs needing help, too. "And I have little faith in Nance Drubeck's helping with *anything*," she muttered to herself. "Lord, if You have an answer to all this, please let me know!" The strain of Willie's disappearance and the loss of Nance's baby was telling on her.

Clell Dobbs had gone upstairs, and she heard his deep voice as he talked to the sick man. Then she heard Clell's footsteps as he clumped across the room and knocked on Nance's door. She couldn't make out what they were saying, but several times she heard Nance's shrill voice in protest.

Barbara had finished the ironing and went to hang up the clothes. Christmas was only two weeks away, and she wondered what gifts to give the boys. The money Clell paid for his board and room helped buy beans, sugar, coffee and cornmeal, but not much else.

She rolled out dough for several dried apple pies and stirred the jack rabbit stew on the back of the stove. As she got out a panful of turnips to scrape, she heard someone coming hesitantly down the stairs. Clell would be waiting for his supper soon.

"Guess I can scrape them turnips for ya," Nance's sullen voice sounded behind her, and Barbara whirled around. Nance stood there, her brown stringy hair combed and tied back with a red ribbon, and her face scrubbed and shining. She wore a green nondescript house dress that looked quite becoming on her. In a wink she had snatched the knife from Barbara's hands.

"You . . . Nance?" Barbara stared at the girl, then caught herself. "Oh, I'm sorry. Of course."

The girl pressed her lips into a tight line, and at first there was only the sharp sound of scraping.

"You . . . been mighty decent to me," Nance began. "Guess I oughtta do somethin' for you. Did . . . did Clell Dobbs tell you I . . . I'm s'posed to change that man's dressin's every day and bring up his food?"

Barbara gulped. *Dear Clell,* she thought. *He really must've laid down the law!* "Oh, he said he thought you might. I'm glad you're so much better. You're looking very pretty, you know." Barbara smiled a little. "You've lost the pallor you had when you were pregnant."

"Let's forget about that!" Nance snapped. "Clell says if I don't pull my weight around here he'll ship me off to . . . to Abilene or some other God-forsaken place." She looked around the room. Homey aromas were emanating from the food on the stove, and the kitchen floor was scrubbed and clean. "Ya know, it's kinda . . . nice here. I . . . I ain't very anxious to go back to my ol' line of work, ya know."

"No, of course not. I love my home and my family. Yet, lately it's been very hard for me to . . . to manage things. If only you'd take over nursing Ed Curtis, with Willie gone—"

"Any word of him?"

"No." Barbara shook her head. "But I've not given up hope. God is still able." She waited for Nance's snappy response at the mention of God, but the girl was quiet.

Clell came downstairs with his coat over his arm, "I've got to run to the shop for awhile, but I'll be back later." The he pulled on his wraps and left.

The wind had died, and dusk leaned down as softly as a bird coming to brood.

Nance picked up a plate and filled it with stew, turnips and cornbread. She poured a tin cup of coffee and started for the stairs. Barbara lit the lamps, washed the boys and combed their hair. Charlie would be home soon.

As she set the table, Nance came back down the stairs, her face tight, with the plate half-empty.

"I should'a known," she muttered. "That man up there thinks he's back on the mission field. I wasn't in that room five minutes when he asked if I knew that God loved me! I felt like throwin' that plateful of food in his face!"

Barbara tried to hide her smile. "And what did you tell him?"

Nance glared at her, the green eyes hard and glassy. "I said . . . said it wasn't none of his business. He asked me to give him his Bible from the little apple crate table where Clell had laid it. Then he began to read somethin' about God . . . God commendin' His love toward us. I grabbed that Bible away from him and threw it across the room! That's when I snatched the plate and came back downstairs. He must be perkin' up!"

"At least you haven't lost your spunk either," Barbara said with a twinkle in her eyes. "For awhile I thought you'd given up on life."

"I've a notion not to go back up there to look after him. If all he's gonna do is preach—"

"That's his job, Nance. He'll pursue his calling just as you pursue yours."

Nance eyed her shrewdly. "I . . . I've about decided not to go back to my old . . . life. But my problem is . . . I don't know what to do."

Barbara heard Charlie's horse galloping toward the barn, and she glanced at the clock.

"Well, why not stay with us until something turns up for you? I can use your help. With the nursing, you know."

Nance glanced at her sharply. "You sure do look poorly right now. Let me think about it."

Breathing a sigh of relief, Barbara thought, *She's beginning to come around, Lord. That's one answer to prayer. Now, if only Willie would come home . . .*

CHAPTER 8

$\mathcal{M}$id-December of 1872 was bitterly cold. There was a smell of snow in the overcast sky as a raw north wind whined in the dry grasses through the scrub brush along the Smoky Hill River. The stark prairie rolled and dipped toward the horizon until it blended into the lead-colored sky. Sleet crackled in the wind as the skies spat icy crystals into the frigid air.

Barbara struggled through the hard days of caring for the boys, cooking the meals and washing for her growing household.

In spite of all her grumbling, Nance Drubeck faithfully carried plates of food upstairs to the injured Ed Curtis and changed the dressings on his shoulder, but that was all she did. She was growing prettier every day, Barbara had noticed. The hardness in the green eyes seemed to melt, and her long, brown hair was combed and tied back neatly with a perky ribbon. The tightness around her mouth had smoothed. When she smiled—which was rare—her face seemed to glow.

Once when Barbara mentioned the tiny baby born a few weeks before, Nance had snapped with anger.

"I don't want to talk about it! The kid's gone and I'm glad."

"But if you'd seen how beautiful she looked, with that dark hair and tiny smile—"

"No! Just forget it, will ya?" she retorted as her green eyes narrowed.

Barbara had hoped that the pain deep down inside Nance's heart had eased some regarding the child's birth, but apparently she was still hurting.

Yet most of the time, the girl seemed more relaxed than when she first came to their house. *If only she'd accept the love we try to offer her,* Barbara thought. But she stayed up in her room as though her only job was to look after Ed Curtis.

Clell Dobbs came and went, faithfully keeping the water pails filled and the wood box full, except on days when his work kept him late at the store.

Charlie often dragged home from the ranch feeling more dead than alive. Caring for the stock during the bitter cold seemed to sap the young vitality that had been so much a part of him. His warm smile and hearty laughter were hardly evident.

Barbara began to feel as though she lived in a vacuum. She rarely had contact with the residents of Ellsworth, aside from the boarders in her house. As the cold weather kept her and the boys inside more often, and the shorter days came and went with such monotony, she couldn't tell one day from the next.

Now and then she climbed the stairs heavily to check on the patient. Ed Curtis, in spite of the wound in his shoulder, was always cheerful. Today he was sitting up in bed with his Bible open on his lap. Barbara noticed how handsome he was, with neat sandy hair and gray eyes that crinkled with laugh lines. She desperately needed his soothing words, his serenity.

"Sit down, Barbara," he said, pointing to the crude apple crate beside the bed. "Do you know what I've been feasting on today? Isaiah 43. God says,

> Fear not: for I have redeemed thee, I have called
> thee by thy name; thou art mine.
>
> When thou passest through the waters, I will be

with thee; and through the rivers, they shall not
overflow thee: when thou walkest through the fire,
thou shalt not be burned; neither shall the flame
kindle upon thee.

"Those are comforting words, Barbara. Think about them
today!"

"Oh, Ed," she gasped, "right now everything's so dismal and
dreary. Charlie's working so hard, and Willie's strange disappearance without a trace, my own constant tiredness, not to
mention Nance Drubeck's bitter attitude . . . I almost despair."

"That's when one needs an extra measure of grace. Just relax
and let the Lord carry you." His gray eyes shone with quiet
confidence.

"I know the Lord has called me to minister to the Klamaths.
Yet I never know from one day to the next if I'll be alive, for
they are sometimes hostile and so slow to respond to God's
love."

He closed his eyes for a moment, and Barbara envied his
serenity.

Then his face crinkled into a smile. "Although I've left the
Klamaths for awhile, the Lord has given me another mission.
And that's to share God's love with Miss Drubeck."

"Which she resents with a passion!" Barbara burst out.
"She's lived a very wayward sort of life, you know. She can't
see how God can love her."

"Then we must continue to try to convince her."

Barbara nodded and rose to her feet, then made her way
slowly down the stairs. She stoked the burning embers in the
stove as Ed's words from the Bible rang in her ears: *I have
redeemed you . . . I have called you by your name . . .*

I haven't always been as kind as I could be to Nance, she
admitted to herself. *But she isn't the easiest person in the
world to love. Right now, I must remind myself that God has
forgiven us in spite of our faults, and in spite of my cir-
cumstances, He has not forgotten me.*

Whenever Clell was kept at the drugstore after work, the

pile of wood behind the stove dwindled, as it had today. Now the fuel was almost gone.

"We need more wood," she said to the boys. "and I'll have to go after it myself. Will you be good while I'm out?"

Danny jumped up. "Momma, let me bring it in. I'm a big boy now. I'm learning to read 'n everything!"

"Oh, bless you, son!" Barbara said, hugging him. "But are you sure?"

"Sure, I'm sure. Just let me try."

Reluctantly she bundled him into his warm coat and cap and picked up the wood basket. "Fill it only half full, Danny. That's all you can manage. Momma's so proud of you," she added, feeling guilty in sending him out to bring in the wet chunks of wood for the stove.

"Me help, too!" Jem shrieked, pulling on Barbara's skirt. She let Danny out quietly and picked up Jem and held him.

"When you're as big as Danny, you can help. Tell you what, Jem. Why don't you bring Momma some potatoes from the lean-to for our supper?"

"Taters wiff gravy?"

"I'll fix them with gravy, if your father comes home with some milk so I can make them that way."

He went obediently to the potato bin in the lean-to and brought them in, one at a time.

As Barbara glanced out the frosty south window for a glimpse of Danny's figure with the wood basket, she gasped. He was tugging the half-filled basket, inching it almost imperceptibly over the frozen ground. She threw on her wraps to help him, and braced herself to avoid a fall on the way out. Cautiously she stepped over the hard earth. Slowly and carefully, she bent over and grabbed hold of a handle on the basket and helped Danny push and tug it toward the kitchen door. Her heavy body strained to keep her balance. Several times she almost fell, and her back hurt from the strain more than ever. Finally they reached the door, and with more pushing and grunting and yanking, they slid the wood basket into the lean-to.

Barbara panted as she staggered toward a chair in the

kitchen. She glanced at the Seth Thomas clock. It was nearly time for Charlie to come home, but she was almost too tired to finish preparing the supper. Her heart pounded and she placed one hand on her abdomen. *Lord, please help me not to hurt my baby. It's still three months until it's due.*

"Danny," she whispered raggedly, "would you please go upstairs and tell Nance to come down?"

Jem snuggled against her and began to whimper. *Oh, dear God, please let Jem calm down. I can't pick him up now.* She stroked his sandy hair and crooned softly until he grew quiet and went back to his play corner.

Nance followed Danny down the stairs, her face puckered into a frown. "Whatcha want? It's not time to eat yet, is it?"

"No, Nance," Barbara said testily. "But I need help. I . . . I did more then I should, helping Danny bring in some stove wood. Could you please . . . peel the potatoes?"

Nance's facial muscles worked into a scowl. "You ain't havin' your baby, are ya? I sure don't know—"

"No, I don't think so. But I'm exhausted. Clell and Charlie will be hungry when they come in. I . . . just can't . . . move."

With a bewildered frown, Nance picked up a paring knife and began to scrape the potatoes, attacking them with a vengeance.

"I thought I was just s'posed to nurse that . . . that *missionary* up there," she said in a derogatory voice. "You said—"

"I know what I said, Nance. But today I'm too tired." She turned her face expectantly toward the door and closed her eyes.

Oh, Dear God, where are You?

When thou passest through the rivers they shall not overflow you . . . through the fire. . . . I have redeemed you . . . I have called you by your name.

She opened here eyes and groped for her thoughts. *Where was Charlie? It was long past his usual hour to come home.*

Clell Dobbs' short little figure bobbed into the kitchen, and eyed Barbara sharply. She continued to sit in her chair, too weary to move.

"I'm sorry I was kept at the store," he said apologetically. He glanced at the water pails. "Let me go after the water right away."

"There wasn't even enough to fix coffee," Nance grumbled when he left. "Well, at least I won't have to go upstairs and listen to that man's preachin' for awhile. He's still hittin' me about God lovin' me."

"And he's right," Barbara said. "I need to remind myself of that more often. It's so easy to forget."

Barbara glanced anxiously at the clock. Charlie should've been home almost two hours ago. Jem began to fret and whimper again.

"Why don't you give the boys some cornbread and molasses? They're starved. There's no sign of Charlie."

"You don't s'pose he disappeared like Willie did, do you?" Nance snorted. "Not that I'd blame him if he took out, too. If I knew where to go, I wouldn't stick around here, either!" With a grimace she fixed two pieces of cornbread and handed them to the boys. "Now start eatin'!"

"We gotta pray first," Danny protested, and bowed his head and mumbled a simple prayer.

"Oh, for land's sakes!" Nance snorted.

Barbara faced Nance. "But you do have a place here with us, you know." She paused to listen. *Was that a horse galloping toward the shed?*

Clell bobbed in carrying the water pails. After he set them on the kitchen floor, he got out the plates and set the table.

With a loud stomping, Charlie flung open the door and came in. His face looked red as a frosted apple and his nose like a ripe sandhill plum. *Oh, dear Charlie—thank God, you're here.* Barbara closed her eyes.

"I'm sorry I was so late, but some of the cattle broke out and we had to get them back into the corral," he said, peeling off his wraps. He looked at her strangely. "Barbara, you all right?"

She opened her eyes and tried to smile, "I am now. But—"

"Momma and me dragged in a basket of wood," Danny said proudly. "I guess she's kinda tired. It was awful hard."

"And I was late comin' home to help," Clell added.

Nance snorted, and began to dish out the boiled potatoes. Charlie placed his arms around Barbara and hugged her tight.

"Oh, my darling," he whispered softly against her hair. "You've had entirely too much to do. I promise you that before too long you'll have a big house with a fireplace in every room, and our own pump for water. It won't be as grand as your plantation home, but it will be better than what we have now!"

Barbara's eyes roved around the shabby kitchen looking at the uncurtained windows, the cold, bare floor, and she shook her head feebly. *Maybe I'm too tired right now, but somehow I can't believe him.*

CHAPTER 9

*T*wo days before Christmas, heavy snow packed the roadways. Thin ice glassed the surfaces of the small creeks and the Smoky Hill River ran black and sluggish under the ice. Prairie chickens perched bravely on the hitching posts or floundered in the deep drifts.

Barbara had worried for days about Christmas gifts for the boys. She knew they would welcome anything to supplement the splintery wooden blocks from the lumberyard Willie had brought home months before. *Willie!* A pain knifed through her as she thought of her congenial brother-in-law's mysterious disappearance. She had prayed so many times for his safe return, but it was as though the earth had opened up and swallowed him.

She'd never forget the Christmas at Pawnee Rock when Mame and Henry Probst had given Willie a shaggy brown pup. Mogie had been his constant companion for over six years.

Ed Curtis had nearly recovered from his wounds, and he came downstairs often to entertain the boys with stories from the Bible. Today he had related the story of the birth of Christ, for they could never get their fill of the drama of the nativity.

"Did the sheep tickle the baby Jesus with their curly tails?" Danny wanted to know. "And why did they stay in a barn?"

"Remember, there was no room for them in the inn—the

hotel in Bethlehem—since many folks had come to pay their taxes," Ed explained carefully. "But Mary and Joseph didn't seem to mind. It was quite cozy there in the straw among the gentle animals. The shepherds took care of their sheep on the hillside, just as your father looks after his cattle. Then the angels came and told them the good news of Jesus' birth."

"Jesus can sleep in Jem's bed," Jem said wistfully, "Not on a straw pillow."

Ed smiled. "I'm sure He'd have been very happy to sleep in your bed if He were here. What Jesus wants today is room in our hearts. That's why He came."

Nance, coming into the kitchen from upstairs, paused with a delicate snort. "Not many folks seem to be askin' Him in, in these parts."

"You're right. But that doesn't keep God from loving us anyway," he countered.

Just then the kitchen door burst open and Clell Dobbs ambled in, carrying two cardboard boxes. They were so large that they nearly obscured Clell's short figure.

Barbara turned away from the stove where she was frying jack rabbit for lunch. She took one look at the boxes and squealed.

"Oh, look! One's from Uncle Daniel's family and the other's from Bitsy!"

"Well, it looks like your worries are over. Better take them into the bedroom before the boys get too curious," Ed suggested quietly.

She threw a grateful glance at him as he drew the boys' attention away from the boxes and began the story of the wisemen.

Snatching up the box from Marion Centre, Barbara carried it to the bedroom while Nance followed with the other. With trembling fingers Barbara untied the cord and tore away the wrappings. Out spilled a tangle of caps and mittens. The knitted caps had obviously come from Aggie's capable fingers. And wrapped in newspapers were two small wooden horses Josh had carved from soft cottonwood limbs. Barbara exclaimed over each item as she held it up. Those blessed cousins, Aggie and Josh!

Nance was already pulling the cord from Bitsy's box. As Barbara whisked away the red tissue paper she gasped. There were books—a neat stack of readers for Danny, including *Black Beauty* and *The Little Brown Bunny*. Sandwiched underneath were several novels, among which were *Uncle Tom's Cabin*, the *Indian Lover*, and the latest copy of *Webster's American Dictionary of the English Language*. Tucked in the bottom were several old issues of *The Manhattan Mercury*.

Tears stung Barbara's eyes at these treasures. Dear Bitsy! She must have realized how starved Barbara was for reading material.

Nance snatched up two of the novels. "I hope ya don't mind."

"As if I have time to read," Barbara said with a wan smile.

The best part of it was that the boys would receive gifts after all.

Suddenly she sniffed. The jack rabbit! She hurried back to the kitchen and yanked the skillet from the front burner just before it scorched. Then she filled a gray enameled kettle with water and dumped in a generous amount of dried corn.

Her step was light as she set the table. *Let Nance read the novels. At least, she'd keep out of Ed Curtis' way.* Silently, Clell had brought in more water and left the house. Nance stood near the stairway door, paging through one of the books.

Ed eyed Barbara with amusement. "I can see that whatever came in those boxes lifted your spirits. I'd prayed just this morning that you'd have a special day."

"Humph! Those boxes were on the way long before you said your prayers!" Nance scoffed. "How can you give credit to God?"

" 'Before you call, I will answer,' Isn't that what the Bible says?"

"All I wanted was for the boys to have a good Christmas,"

Barbara said as she poured cream into the kettle of steaming corn. "And I'm very grateful. Ed, I'm glad you're doing so well. Nance, lunch is ready in a minute."

Ed set Jem down and rose to his feet. "After Christmas I must head back to St. Louis, as I'd planned before that bullet interrupted my journey."

Nance laid the novels on the steps and glanced up sharply at his words. *No doubt,* Barbara thought, *she'll be glad to see an end to his "preachin'."*

"You won't go away, will you, Mr. Ed?" Danny said tearfully, "When Christmas is over?"

"I'm afraid so, Danny. Your mother and Nance have taken such good care of me that I'm all fixed up. I must go back home and get ready for my work among the Klamath Indians."

"Klammy bad Indians?" Jem asked.

"We're all sinners, and Christ died for everyone. That's what I want to tell the Klamaths."

"I wonder if bad Indians took Uncle Willie away," Danny mused aloud.

Barbara looked sharply at Ed. A puzzled frown ribbed his forehead; then he shook his head lightly.

"Wherever he is, we know he's in God's care," he said simply.

Apparently Nance figured that since Ed Curtis no longer needed her care, her job was over, for she stayed upstairs all day with the novels Bitsy had sent, leaving Barbara to struggle with the work.

On Christmas Eve Charlie came home early. His gray shawl was wrapped tightly around his shoulders and his cap was pulled over his forehead as he stomped into the house. Clell had shoveled a path through the snow to the front door. Barbara sighed. The family had made plans to attend the program at the little church near Thompson's Creek, but she was almost too tired to dress the boys. Still, she knew Danny had worked hard on the song he was to sing.

Charlie helped dress Jem and Danny and slicked down their hair. Barbara pulled on her shabby green bombazine that had seen so many years of wear and had been let out in the seams to accommodate her pregnancy. She patted it snugly over her middle and tried to coax a few curls over her forehead.

"Oh, fudge!" she fumed, whacking a hairbrush through the limp strands. "I look like a stuffed sausage and my hair refuses to behave. All I can do is twist it into a plain knot and forget how frowsy I look!"

"You'll always be my beautiful belle, Barbara," Charlie said softly as he dressed Jem in his coat and cap. "Don't forget — you're the mother of two strapping sons and expecting another child in three months."

"Some belle! If the boys weren't involved in the service tonight, I'd stay home with Nance. I'm so tired."

"I know. But you'll do fine, darling."

Already she could hear Clell outside with the team and a buckboard on runners from the livery stable that jingled and clanked as it creaked over the snow. Charlie had banked the fire and set the eggs, the bread box and a thawed-out piece of side meat on chairs in front of the stove. Then he took the boys out to the sleigh and tucked them under the buffalo robes.

Barbara had just pulled on her coat, wrapped the shawl around her head and jerked on her mittens, when Nance Drubeck came down the stairs. She gasped. The girl looked stunning in a soft black velvet gown with a revealing neckline and a narrow gold belt around her slim waist. Her hair was upswept and glittered and gleamed with tortoiseshell combs. A pair of long gold earrings dangled from her ear lobes.

"Nance, are you . . . going with us? Or—"

"Why not? You've begged me to go to church so many times I thought I'd go. Is that so awful? I do wanna hear Danny sing. Or won't there be room in the sled?" She slipped into a shabby fur coat and flung a long red scarf over her head.

"Why . . . I'm sure there's room," Barbara stammered. *Now, what was the real reason Nance Drubeck decided to go to church?* "Are you going to be warm enough? We'd better hurry. The others are waiting," Barbara said.

Nance pushed her way in front of Barbara and stepped

gingerly through the snow, then scrambled into the sled next to Ed Curtis. Charlie waited for Barbara, and clutched her in his arms as he helped her into the sleigh. Then he wrapped a robe around her.

Clell clucked to the team and the sleigh skimmed over the snow-packed white country road that shimmered under the pale light of the yellow prairie moon.

Minutes later, they reached the little frame church that crouched alone beside the sleepy creek. Lantern light spilled from the windows, and with a yell and splattering of snow, Clell urged the team to a stop.

The little church was already filling with farmers who had crossed the snowy prairie for the Christmas Eve service. Once inside, Barbara drew off the boys' wraps and followed Charlie into the sanctuary. Several women raised their chins when they saw the over-dressed Nance Drubeck prance down the aisle after Barbara. Of course, she was glad Nance had finally condescended to come to church, and she wondered again if the girl had an ulterior motive. *It couldn't be Ed Curtis, could it? Ridiculous!* Nance couldn't stand his constant reference to the Lord. The girl held herself aloof from the small crowd as she slipped into the rough pews and spread her black velvet skirt over her shapely legs.

At Pastor Sternberg's beckoning, Danny marched to the platform. In a clear, sing-song voice he began his lullaby:

> Little baby in a manger, I love you.
> Lying here to earth a stranger, I love you.
> Wisemen saw the star and answered, "I love you."
> Shepherds heard the angles singing, "I love you."

Tears filled Barbara's eyes as she watched her son participate in the evening's program. *I'm so proud of him,* she thought. If Willie could only hear him. Tears stung her eyes again, knowing it would take a miracle for him to return. Jem, on Charlie's lap, took in everything with his big eyes watching all around.

An hour later they were back at the shabby two-story house with each of the boys clutching an orange and a bag of hard candies that someone had provided for the handful of children after the program. Wearily, Barbara dragged herself to the bedroom to get the boys ready for bed. Suddenly Danny spied the gifts on the shelf which she had forgotten to hide.

"Oh, Momma, look! Books! And . . . and horsies!"

There was no stopping them now. Instead of waiting until Christmas morning, Barbara nodded to Charlie and shooed them into the kitchen. She took down the gifts and followed, then dropped ponderously into a chair. Charlie stoked the fire until it snapped and crackled with warmth. Nance had shrugged out of her fur coat and stood before the fire, warming her hands.

"Your song sounded nice, Danny," she said. "I didn't know you could sing like that."

Danny didn't say anything. He was much too engrossed with his books. Barbara thought, *Nance is really behaving like a decent human being*.

Clell Dobbs stomped in from stabling the team and drew out half a dozen red apples from his coat pockets.

"Here. Apples anyone?"

Jem had crawled sleepily into Barbara's lap, clutching his little carved horse, and she relaxed. Her tiredness seemed to suddenly dissipate as Charlie, Clell, Ed and Nance pulled up chairs near the stove to garner in the warmth while munching their apples. Danny scrambled around, hardly knowing what to do first: play with his horse or read his books.

To Barbara it seemed that the simple, yet wonderful events of this Christmas Eve enfolded them like a gentle benediction from God, and she sighed with contentment. Only Willie was missing.

CHAPTER 10

*B*arbara awoke to a bright clear morning. Dazzling glimpses of blue sky rifted between torn white clouds, and she stirred under the warm covers and blinked. It promised to be a warm day, turning the streets slushy again. A brief thaw the day after Christmas had melted most of the snow, leaving everything sodden underfoot.

She dressed quickly and hurried to the kitchen. Charlie had left an hour ago for the ranch, and she stoked the dying embers in the old black stove.

Ed Curtis planned to leave for St. Louis on the eleven o'clock train, and she set a kettle of water on the stove to start a hot, nourishing breakfast. Already she heard his stirring upstairs. Presently he thumped down the steps lugging his shabby valise.

Beaming with his merry face crinkled in laugh lines, he drew a deep breath. "To tell the truth, Barbara, I wasn't very happy about that bullet in my shoulder, since I should've been home weeks ago. But when Clell Dobbs brought me here 'n said I could share his room, and that Nancy Drubeck had nothing to do but play nurse, what else could I do? I'm sorry if I've been a drag, but it's been a real pleasure to have been a part of your household these past weeks."

Barbara stirred the porridge and dipped coffee from its tin

can into the gray pot. "If Clell hadn't asked Nance to look after you, we'd never made it. I've not been well myself, but the Lord has given grace and strength."

"I know, and I appreciate all you've done. Your husband could've thrown me out for burdening you even more when you already had so much. But that funny, indomitable, lovable Clell Dobbs certainly pitched in and helped. God bless him!"

Barbara nodded. "What amazes me is that Nance did her job, faithfully keeping your bandages changed. She was most uncooperative when she came last fall."

"Well, that's Clell's doing. I overheard him tell her she had no business staying with decent folks like you, and he was going to insist she pack up and leave if she didn't look after me. I guess she appreciates you more than you know, Barbara."

"Appreciates me!" Barbara flared. "She's been most contrary! Well, I only hope we've helped her . . . somehow. Here's your breakfast, Ed."

He pulled out a chair and sat down at the table. Barbara heard Jem stirring and she hurried into the bedroom. *Ed was right,* she thought. *Clell had known how to make the girl toe the line.* As he had said, the man was funny, indomitable—and lovable. She didn't know how they would've managed without him.

Time went by quickly. At the first whistle of the locomotive, Ed slipped into his coat and picked up Jem for a quick hug.

"You be a good boy, Jeremy. And don't ever forget me!"

Danny ran for Ed's outstretched arms. "I sure won't. You tell the goodest Bible stories!"

"Just don't you forget them," he said after a brief hug. "And you, Barbara. God bless you and Charlie, and make you a blessing to all who enter this home."

He paused, turning at the sound on the stairs. Nance had come down wearing a simple cotton print dress that was almost the same shade of green as her eyes. Her hair was combed neatly and tied back with a green silk ribbon. *She looks like an innocent child,* Barbara thought. *Sweet and vulnerable.*

Nance started as she caught sight of Ed's valise. "Oh, you're leavin' this mornin'?"

He reached out his hand and smiled. "That's my train telling me to hurry if I want to catch a ride to St. Louis. Thank you again, Nancy, for the good care you gave me. Without your help I probably would still be in Clell's bed upstairs." He reached out his other hand to Barbara, and said softly,

"Let me give you a verse from Psalm 121: 'The LORD shall preserve thy going out and thy coming in from this time forth, and even for evermore.'

"And for you, Nancy, 'The Lord shall preserve thee from all evil: he shall preserve thy soul.' These verses are my prayers for you. And now, I must go."

Quickly he snatched up his bag and hurried out the door. As it banged behind him, Barbara stood at the window and watched him stride briskly down the muddy path that led to the station.

Then she drew a deep breath, "He was so congenial when he was mending. I just know we'll miss him!"

Nance, who had stood silently, tossed her head. "He *had* to have his last word from the Bible!" she snorted. Then she drew a small Bible from her dress pocket. "Look what he left behind. It's got my name in it. As if he thinks I'll read it!" She plopped down on the steps and twisted her face into a grimace.

"Nance, Ed Curtis is first and foremost a Christian gentleman, and his main concern is for people to know and love the Lord. You know that!"

"Well, if he wasn't so religious I could've almost fallen for him. But, of course, his kind would never take a second look at the likes of me. So why'd he leave this Holy Bible behind for me?"

"I'm sure he hopes you'll read it, Nance."

"Humph!" she snorted again. "That's what *he* thinks!" Then she whirled around and scudded up the stairs again.

The house seemed strangely quiet with Ed's leaving. Clell came in from work early and immediately took the water pails and left.

Barbara had put the freshly ironed clothes away and sat down in a chair for a brief moment of rest. With a scoot Jem was on her lap.

"Momma, Ed come back? Tell more 'tory?"

"No, dear. He is well again, so he had to go away." She paused to tousle his hair and kissed his neck.

"Now Unca Willie come back?"

Barbara sighed. "I . . . don't know. We'll have to wait and see."

"He's been gone a long time, Momma," Danny said. "But with Ed Curtis here, I didn't miss Uncle Willie quite so much. Now that Ed is gone—"

"Why don't you wash up for supper? Momma will put the prairie chickens on to fry in a minute."

Wearily, she got up from her chair and moved toward the stove. *If only Nance would be more helpful,* she thought. *She must still be reading the novels Bitsy sent.* She shook her head thoughtfully and reflected. *I remember when I came to Marion Centre from Atlanta in 1863, I was too prissy to help Aunt Prudy and the cousins. All I did was devour my cheap novels.* Again she shuddered to think of the similarity between her and Nance in this regard. *What a difference the Lord has made in me!* she rejoiced.

The next several days passed in a blur. The New Year of 1873 stole in with a fresh blast of cold air. Snow was frozen solid on the small panes of the windows, and the west windows were covered with gunny sacks Charlie had tacked over them. Every evening Barbara brought the milk and eggs from the lean-to into the kitchen and set them before the stove. In the morning the windows were opaque with white whiskers of frost and, more than likely, the water was frozen in the pails.

One day passed like the one before, and Barbara dragged herself through the long, cold hours on leaden feet. Nance seemed to know when the meals were on the table, and she also saw to it that the little round stove upstairs was supplied with fuel. Clell came and went, congenial as ever, his bald, shiny head darting like a bird's when he talked. Barbara had almost stopped praying for Willie. He seemed to have been swallowed up as though he'd never existed.

Charlie came home from the ranch, day after day, tired from looking after the stock, and fell asleep the minute he had finished his supper.

When Bitsy's letters came in the mail, the bleak, drab days seemed brighter. She wrote:

Dear Barbie,

I guess it's high time I write you again. I told you about the little house Merritt and I moved into when we settled in Manhattan. It's a nifty little cottage down the street from the college. Merritt loves his teaching at Bluemont. I still can't believe I'm a mother! Remember how flighty I always was? Our children are like a pair of honeybees, always buzzing around. I call them Buzz and Honey—never mind which is which! Well, with Bluemont being a 'cow college', we have plenty of milk and everything here but buffalo! Sometimes, though, I get homesick for the little cabin by the Cottonwood with Vange and Aggie and Josh—and you, of course. How I wish I could see you all again in person . . .

Barbara paused and sighed. Yes, those were precious days, and she missed them all dreadfully. She'd so hoped here in Ellsworth she would have friends, but there were few women in town with whom she wanted to associate. Besides, she was always so tired, and her back hurt constantly after she took care of the family's needs. If only March would come and the new baby would arrive, perhaps her days would be brighter.

A week after New Year's Day, a loud insistent knock sounded on the kitchen door at mid-afternoon. *Now who would come for a social call?* she wondered. Slowly Barbara moved across the room and opened it. There, outlined in the doorway, was the familiar blurry figure that Barbara recognized instantly.

"Mame!" She shrieked as she pulled the plump, bouncy woman into the kitchen, with her neatly mended jacket and the gray, bobbing topknot. "It's really you, Mame Probst? Oh, I can't believe it!"

"Yes, it's me—no more, no less. Let me look at you, Barb'ra." She took Barbara's shoulders in her gloved hands and stared at her, then she hugged her with a gruff bear hug. "My, you've growed up. Not that sassy little snippet you was when you left Pawnee Rock. But you look peaked. Oh, you're in a family way, I see."

Barbara helped Mame pull off the jacket and led her toward the stove.

"Here. Warm your hands. You must be almost frozen."

"Well, I ain't that cold. They keep the stages warm with hot bricks. How long has it been since you left Western Kansas for Atlanta with your cousin? Six, seven years?" She looked around the room. Jem and Danny came in sleepily from the bedroom.

Barbara laughed. "I guess you didn't know. We have two sons. They're just up from their naps."

"Two young'uns, you say?"

"Yes. And, did you know, Nance is staying with us?"

Mame snorted as she rocked back and forth on her heels. "Yes. She wrote me about the fix she was in. I'm s'prised she came here, knowin' what kind'a person she is."

Barbara bit her lip sharply. "She . . . she was booted out of her job when her boss discovered she was going to have a baby. She needed a place to stay . . . and we took her in."

"The young'un?"

"It . . . was stillborn nearly two months ago. A beautiful little girl. Nance is still here."

Mame looked boldly around the room. "I hope she pitches in and helps with the work?"

"Well," Barbara hesitated. "She nursed a man we took in who'd been shot while he was traveling on the stage from Denver. He left not long ago. I . . . I manage, and Clell Dobbs lends a hand. He . . . he works in the drug store and asked if he could stay here, rather than in one of the hotels. He's been a lifesaver, carrying water and fuel and running errands."

"What about the young'un what lived with you—Willie or somethin'? What's he up to?"

With a deep sigh, Barbara told Mame about Willie's strange disappearance and how they had heard nothing of his whereabouts.

"It's as though he was swallowed up in a giant hole in the ground. We don't know—" Tears sprang to Barbara's eyes and she choked on her words.

"Now, now, don't you fret none. I feel he'll show up one of these days. Just be patient. Tell you what, Barb'ra. I'm to start work in the Ol' Reliable's kitchen in a week, and I can see you need a good rest. Let me look after your family while you go to bed. Maybe you'll get rested up 'fore your baby comes. That should be in about—"

"March. Sometimes I don't see how I'll be able to hold out that long."

"You will. Just let ol' Mame take over and don't you worry about a thing. Your boys'll have to mind me. I'll even get my niece to do somethin' around here, or my name ain't Mame Probst!"

Barbara smiled. Knowing Mame, she didn't doubt it. She'd probably move furniture around, too. Mame had always been as gritty as sandpaper and snappy as a turtle. She "ruled the roost," as Henry Probst, bless his soul, always said.

The next hour was a riot of Mame's shrill bossing, loving and "managing" just as she always had.

"You young'uns, let your Ma go to bed" she scolded Danny and Jem when they tried to climb on Barbara's lap. "She's all tuckered out with too much to do."

When Nance came downstairs and saw her aunt, her green eyes widened. "So you did what you said you'd do, Aunt Mame," she said tartly. "You always threatened to come and straighten me out. Well, I'm perfectly happy right here, the way I am."

"Shame on you, Nance Drubeck. Can't you see Barb'ra's

ready to drop? Why ain't you helpin' her?"

Nance arched one eyebrow. "Oh, I did nurse that mission-ary. Anyway, she seems to think it's her 'Christian duty' to take people in, so why spoil it for her?" she scoffed.

"We'll see about that!" Mame's voice was short. "Now look in the lean-to for some vittles. We're fixin' grub for supper—you and me!" She whirled around and stirred the dying embers in the stove. "Barb'ra, that shelf oughtta be moved over to that corner. It'd be handier there."

By the time Clell came in, Mame had moved it into the corner. Clell bowed and reached out a gloved hand. "Please to meet you, Miz Probst. Let me help you with that," he offered as Mame stacked the last of the dry goods back on the bottom shelf.

Charlie also seemed glad to see Mame when he came home. "How did you escape the Cheyennes who stormed over the Santa Fe Trail that horrible September of '66?" he asked after he had given her a warm embrace.

Mame grunted as she toyed with the biscuit dough. "When them so'jers from Fort Larned rode up to warn us, we didn't think the Injuns'd find us in our dugout. Henry was all set to stay. You know how stubborn he was. But I grabbed all I could carry in a feed sack and took out on foot to our root cellar on the other side of the hill. That's where I hid. The yells and ruckus was awful. When it died away, I crept out. They took everythin' worth takin', even my good china. And I found Henry . . . with an arrer through his chest." She paused and sniffed, then shook her head. "Poor Henry! I . . . I set out afoot toward the Fort. Them so'jers came back and buried him. I stayed there at the Fort and took over the cookin' for awhile, then got a job at Dodge, in an eatin' house.

"When I heard from Nance and she said you folks was here. I decided to come and neighbor with you again. I guess you need me right now. God moves in mysterious ways. But I'm sure sorry to hear about poor Willie."

Clell Dobbs was silent, and Barbara noticed his eyes never left Mame's animated face. *Just like Willie,* Barbara thought.

Something about the big, blurry woman had seemed to fascinate people. *All but me . . . when I first met her,* Barbara mused. *How I disliked her at first . . . until she saved Charlie's life when he almost died of pneumonia. As I look back now, I'm sure that God sent her.* Barbara sighed. *It doesn't matter if Mame moves my furniture around again,* she thought, *I'm glad she's here. Dear God, thank You for sending Mame Probst again when I needed her!*

CHAPTER 11

$\mathcal{B}$arbara savored the week of rest that Mame had promised her. To stay in bed and not have a worry about the meals, the laundry, the boys fretting about being cooped up indoors was a taste of heaven. She slept for hours—gentle, healing sleep that poured strength into her tired body. She even indulged in the novels Bitsy had sent for Christmas and saturated herself with the soothing Psalms. Still, she felt guilty because she was doing nothing.

Mame cooked great pots of soup thick with potatoes and parsnips, and swimming with chunks of beef. She baked mounds of pies and loaves of wheat bread, and molasses cookies, and the family gathered around the table with heartier appetites than they had displayed all winter.

When Barbara ventured out of her bed to see how Mame was "managing," the big blurry woman bounced toward her and shooed her back to bed.

"You just rest while you have a chance. Things is gettin' done without you puttin' your nose in the way," she scolded mildly. "Leave the boys to me. They gotta let you rest."

Nance drifted in and out of the kitchen, and Barbara saw her carrying pans of vegetables or piles of laundry. Even the boys seemed cheerful and satisfied.

Oh, it was bliss to do nothing but sleep, rest and relax. *I'd better take advantage of Mame's pampering while I can,* she mused. But she worried that Mame was doing too much. After all, the woman wasn't getting any younger.

When Barbara told her there was no need to wear herself out, she retorted, "Before we leave, Nance and me will wash down the walls, hem up some curtains, and freshen up the whole house." Barbara had never had the money to buy curtains for the kitchen, but by the next morning they had appeared.

"I'm runnin' your house this week, Barb'ra. Didn't I make that clear?" Mame's voice shrilled from the kitchen. "But you can come to the table to eat. Over here," she pointed when Barbara started toward the south end of the room. "I shoved the table by the east window where you can ketch the mornin' sun and look out to the street." She paused again. "Hmm. I trust my cookin's tolerable." She frowned. "Noticed you ain't got an iron cookin' pot."

Barbara sighed, remembering how Mame had grouched about Barbara cooking in an enameled pot instead of iron. Fortunately her enameled pots were a few of the items Charlie had stuffed into the sack before he and Willie had fled from the Indians. She bit back a tart reply, knowing how Mame's gritty comments had always grated at her soul. *But Mame will always be Mame,* she decided—*tactless, and doing things her way.* Yet every stroke of work was a labor of love.

"You're spoiling me, Mame," Barbara sputtered that night. "It's been so long since I've had a chance to be lazy."

The boys obeyed Mame like little angels. Danny "yes-ma'amed" and "no-ma'amed" her until Charlie thought he'd choke with laughter. Mame expected to be obeyed and they soon learned it.

Even Charlie seemed less tense at night when he came in from the ranch. *He must be pleased about my chance to rest,* Barbara thought. Clell Dobbs bobbed in and out of the house, his face always clean-shaven, and even his boots scrupulously clean. The little druggist bowed more than ever that week while Mame "ruled the roost." *She's charmed him along with the others,* Barbara mused. Only Nance seemed morose and uncommunicative, and rebelled at Mame's orders whenever she dared.

The week passed all too quickly. On Sunday afternoon, when Mame carried her shabby valise downstairs and buttoned into her tattered gray jacket, Nance followed her with her own valise packed and ready to depart. She looked up at Barbara with a scowl.

"I told my niece she'll have to move into my room with me at the Ol' Reli'ble," Mame chattered, pulling on her mended gloves. "I don't want her to go back to her old life, and I don't want her botherin' you no more. I think my boss at the hotel will give her a job as cleanin' maid or waitressin'. One reason why we redded up your house was so she'd learn a few things," she added with a smirk.

Tears stung Barbara's eyes as she realized the two women were packed and ready to go. She felt more rested than she'd been in months, but it was high time she took over her own household again.

"Oh, Mame," she cried. "I'll miss you very, very much!"

"Fiddle-faddle. I ain't movin' to the end of the world. Just down the street a block or two. I'll come see you often." She paused and pointed to the largest cooking pot. "There's a big mess of ham 'n bean soup that should last a day or so. And some fresh bread in that stone crock over there. Don't let the boys eat too much fresh butter. It ain't healthy for growin' boys."

"We sure been eating lots of 'lasses cookies," Danny said, smacking his lips.

"Cookie! Cookie!" Jem whimpered, and Mame promptly snatched a handful of round, crunchy pastries from a tin pail for him.

"Better for you than all that butter bread," Mame muttered. "Well, Nance, you ready to tote your bag?"

"I'm sure Clell will be glad to carry your bags when he comes in," Barbara said. "Charlie's gone to check on a stray cow he said hadn't made it back to the corral last night." She paused as a thin smile parted her lips, "I . . . I'm glad we could give you a place to stay when you needed it."

The girl mumbled something that Barbara couldn't understand, but it sounded something like "Just bein' a peck of trouble."

"Well, I promised I'd be at the Ol' Reli'ble to cook breakfast in the mornin'. Just you take it easy now, Barb'ra," Mame cut in. "Me 'n Nance will come by now 'n then to lend a hand. And you young'uns—you be good. Don't give your Ma any trouble after I leave! And there ain't no need for Clell Dobbs to tote our bags. They ain't that heavy."

After hugging the boys briefly, she gave Barbara a quick squeeze. Then she grabbed her shabby valise, clucked to Nance, and they slammed out of the house.

Danny stared at Barbara, and she saw tears lurking in his eyes. "Will you be our Momma again now?"

She gave him a warm hug and sat down in her chair. "Why, I'm always your Momma. No one will ever take that special privilege away from me. It was just that I was so tired, and Mame offered to help so I could catch up on my rest. Now I'm rested up. Mame looked after you just fine, didn't she?"

"She didn't read us any stories," Danny muttered.

"But she did so many other things!"

"Read 'tory, Momma!" Jem clamored, climbing onto her lap with the *Brown Bunny* book.

With a happy sigh, Barbara spent the next half hour with her sons, grateful for the chance to look after them again.

The house seemed almost too quiet without Mame's constant bouncing and thumping around, her boisterous voice echoing through the house. Even Clell remarked about it when he came in for supper that night.

"Well, she sure stirred things up in this house!"

Barbara smiled as she set the table. Clell had said it best.

Charlie stomped into the house, pulled off his wraps and sat down in one of the kitchen chairs. He leaned his head back, and his dark curls tumbled over his forehead as he laced his hands behind his head. A weak smile tugged at his lips.

"I finally found her," he muttered, "after searching all over the range. The critter suddenly appeared on the rim of a knoll, stopped and stared, then trotted away. So I rode up after her. That's when I spotted a small herd down in an arroyo that strayed from a cattle drive. There was no brand on them. She must've joined up with them somehow."

"Which means?" Barbara asked breathlessly.

"Which means we're about 12 cows richer than we were before," he said smiling broadly. "I don't know how they survived the winter—unless they drifted along the ranges and gobbled up stacked hay. They're skinny as a row of fence posts, but we'll fatten them up in time."

Barbara announced supper was ready and Charlie offered a prayer of thanks. The last of Mame's thick bean soup soon disappeared as they sat down to eat, and the peace of the evening sifted over them. The pale light of a winter sunset filtered through the new curtains on the windows and fell like a benediction upon the day. Not a sound broke the stillness except the ticking of the clock, the faint moaning of the draft through the chimney of the stove and the occasional drop of a chunk of wood falling on the grate as the fire burned lower.

During the next several days Barbara resumed her regular work in the house with her replenished energy. Although she missed Mame, she felt a deeper emptiness about Willie's absence. If only Willie would come home!

She was grateful for the new addition to their herd, and she smiled as she bent over the dish pan that Wednesday morning. She wondered how Mame was faring at her new job. Even more, she wondered about Nance Drubeck. The girl had been so self-assured at her old "job" until she had to face some of the consequence of that "line of work." What was her attitude now? Would she stick with her carping Aunt Mame or slip away to another bawdy house? *I don't think I helped her a bit,* Barbara thought dubiously. *But I tried.*

The boys had been restless all morning, pulling on her skirt, demanding, crabbing, yelling, until Barbara threw up her hands. What was wrong with them?

She glanced out the window. The sky was a blaze of blue, with high, cauliflower clouds that seemed to hang motionless. The chill wind of the night had died to a whisper, and the outdoors looked calm and quiet.

She whirled away from the window. "Danny, Jem, you're as restless as a pair of disturbed setting hens, and I have a half a mind to shoo you outdoors for an hour."

"Oh, Momma, can we?" Danny cried, tugging on her arm. "I'll look after Jem real good. I promise."

She hesitated only a moment. The boys had rarely been outside to play in the past few weeks. This was the first mild winter day since December, and they needed to work off steam. Quickly she bundled them into their wraps and opened the door.

"Now don't go any farther than that shed over there," she cautioned. "And Danny, don't take your eyes off Jem for one minute!"

"I said I'd watch him good, Momma," he squealed. "I'm almost seven. We'll be good. I promise."

Anxiously Barbara watched as they scampered down the damp walk, waving their arms and shrieking like a pair of silly geese. *I hope they'll work off some excess energy,* she thought.

As she walked back into the kitchen, she glanced around. It did look fresh and clean, after Nance had scrubbed the soot from the walls and ceiling and wiped the windows until they shined. The crisp checkered curtains gave a cheerful look to the room that had become the heart of their home.

For the first time in months she felt practically like her old self. She almost wished for company to arrive. Of course, she had kept apart from the townsfolk, except to buy a few necessities at Beebe's Store. Maybe after the baby came and spring arrived, life would be more normal—except for Willie's absence. A part of her would always feel empty where her love for her congenial brother-in-law had warmed her heart.

Suddenly, Danny rushed into the house, pulling Jem by one arm, and yelling and screaming with excitement.

"It's Willie—" Danny panted, and Jem echoed, "Unca Willie . . . Unca Willie . . . Unca Willie!"

Barbara turned quickly. "Boys! Boys! Not so loud. Please calm down. You know Willie's away—"

"But he's coming! We seed him. He was walking real slow down that way. He's coming, Momma. He really is!"

She shook her head. For so long she had hoped and prayed. The boys must've seen someone who looked like Willie from a distance. *It just couldn't be true, or could it?*

Danny grabbed her hand and jerked her toward the door. "See, Momma? There he is!"

As she followed his pointed finger, she saw the slow, thin, plodding figure wearing a ragged jacket coming toward the house like a tired old man. And beside him, hanging on his arm stumbled a young Indian girl, her dark hair disheveled, clutching a tattered blanket around her. *But . . . oh, yes, it was Willie!*

Heedless of the cold, Barbara ran to meet him, crying and waving her arms with joy. He stopped and threw his arms around her with a glad cry. A beard covered his once-clean-shaven, freckled face. "Thank God . . . thank God," she breathed over and over.

"Barbara . . . Barbara," Willie whispered hoarsely. "It's so good to be . . . home!"

They clung together, tears raining down their cheeks and mingling together until suddenly Barbara drew away. *The boys!*

"Danny? Jem?"

Danny stood beside her, silently holding Jem's hand and waiting as they both looked from Willie to the Indian girl and to their mother. Willie took hold of the Indian girl's hand again.

"Barbara . . . this is White Lily. She . . . we escaped from the Cheyennes. I brought her home with me. You don't mind, do ya?"

The Indian girl looked about 12 years old. Her face was thin and sad, and gently Barbara placed an arm around the narrow shoulders. She pointed to the door.

"Let's go in where it's warm. And you stay with us as long as you like, White Lily," she said as she ushered her into the kitchen.

Motioning the girl to a chair, Barbara hurried to stoke the fire until it burned into a bright, crackling blaze.

Willie stood in the middle of the room and stared as if devouring the sight of his home from which he had been absent so many weeks. Barbara moved almost dizzily, still in semi-shock, and she pushed him into the other chair. It was still so hard to believe!

Danny approached Willie hesitantly. "It's sure good you got back. I . . . I can read, Uncle Willie. Really, really read! You wanna hear me?"

"Can ya, Danny?" He nodded. "That's great. Oh, it's so good to be back!"

Instantly Willie had both boys in his arms, hugging and stroking their tousled heads.

White Lily covered her face in her hands and sobbed softly. *Surely she must be very tired, and perhaps even afraid,* Barbara thought.

After the boys had settled down, Barbara placed an arm around Willie's shoulders and nuzzled her head against his thin cheek.

"Oh, Willie . . . what happened? Where have you been?"

He grinned sheepishly. "I'm not exactly sure, but I'll tell you as much as I know." She noticed his smile was tired and his color was pale. How weary they both looked!

As much as she wanted to hear the whole story, she thought she would spare him having to tell the story twice, so she placed her fingers softly over his lips. "Later. It's almost time to fix supper. Clell Dobbs said he'd be late, but I pray your brother Charlie won't. You can tell us everything after we eat. You must be hungry. He'll be in soon."

"Clell did come then?"

"Yes. And he's been God's ministering angel."

Her heart pounding, Barbara scurried into the lean-to for a

cut of side beef and a pan of potatoes. Willie leaned back his head wearily, half asleep.

The kitchen grew redolent with the aroma of frying beef and the bubbling of potatoes in the gray enameled kettle. She found some of Mame's boiled apples in the lean-to. The quiet was broken only by the lid thrumming on the kettle and the hiss of meat frying in the pan. A peacefulness she hadn't known in a long time had settled into the kitchen. Danny laid his head against Willie's lap while Jem was over in the corner playing with his carved horse. Willie sighed heavily, almost too tired to speak.

The Osage girl had fallen asleep in her chair, her head buried in her thin arms on the table.

When Barbara heard Charlie's horse gallop up the street, her heart started pounding again. She could hardly wait for him to come indoors.

He stomped into the kitchen and, as usual, he headed for the water pails as if he knew Clell would be late.

Barbara placed a detaining hand on his shoulder. "The water can wait, Charlie. Look who's here!"

Charlie glanced around sharply, then he let out a rebel yell. "Willie! My little brother! Oh, praise God!"

In two quick strides he was standing near the table, grabbing Willie out of his chair and pulling him into his arms.

Barbara was crying so hard she snatched up a tea towel to wipe her eyes.

"Oh, dear Lord . . . dear, dear Lord," she whispered. "You heard. You answered. Thank You!"

CHAPTER 12

*T*he next half hour passed swiftly. White Lily had fallen asleep again at the supper table, and Barbara told Charlie to carry her to the bedroom. No doubt, the girl was completely exhausted.

After filling his plate with food twice and polishing off every last crumb, Willie sat up bravely and seemed to enjoy the comforts of home again. The boys hovered around Barbara's ankles as she cleared away the evening meal. The table was wiped clean, except for Clell's portion which she placed in the warming oven. Then she shooed them to the bedroom and undressed them for bed.

"Tonight we'll thank Jesus for bringing Uncle Willie home safely, won't we?" she said softly to avoid disturbing the sleeping Indian girl on the double bed.

"You didn't wanna believe it was Willie," Danny grouched, trying to stifle a yawn. "But God brought him back, didn't He?"

Barbara kissed the boys and tucked them into the trundle bed, after their prayers. Jem was already asleep. "Yes, He did," she whispered. "I had looked for his return for so long that it was hard to believe when it finally happened. Good night, Danny."

She tiptoed from the room and went quietly back into the kitchen. Clell had just come home. The little pharmacist greeted Willie with a firm handshake. Then Willie pulled off his ragged boots and laid his head on his arms.

"You look all tuckered out, Willie," Clell said. "You can use your old bed. I'll take the one in the south room."

Barbara looked at him quickly. "Willie brought a guest," she said. "The Indian girl is so exhausted we put her on our bed for now. I thought—"

"Sure. She can have Miz Drubeck's room. I'll throw some covers on the floor by Willie's bed for me. But how come—"

Willie grinned a little and Barbara noticed his freckles faintly mottled through his fine beard.

"I guess I'd better tell you."

"You'd better get some rest first, Willie," Charlie said, "however long it takes." He looked at his brother as if in expectation, and Barbara waited, too. She had tried to stifle her curiosity but she was anxious to hear his story.

"After a good night's sleep I'll be fine. But I must tell you first what happened." He drew a deep breath and began. "That day when we delivered the lumber and I helped unload it, I was to ride out to the Comstocks' spread with the nails they needed to finish their barn. I was lopin' along when Queenie stepped into a prairie dog hole and threw me. I really don't know what happened after that, for I must'a hit my head on a rock and it knocked me out cold.

"When I came to, I was a-layin' on the floor of a cave with my hands and feet tied with leather thongs. I don't know how long I was out. I couldn't remember a thing when I came to. I didn't even remember my own name, or where I was from— nothin'."

"Amnesia," Clell muttered almost under his breath.

"Am—? Whatever it was. No matter how I tried, I couldn't recall a thing. Injuns—Cheyennes they was—chattered and grunted, but I couldn't understand a word. They treated me quite decent, though. Gave me meat and water. But there was nothin' to do but lay there day after day, tryin' to think and remember." He shook his head. "The days dragged on and on. When it got colder, they moved me deeper into the cave. They kept a warm fire goin' so I never really got very cold. I wore my jacket all the time.

"Suddenly I heard weepin' and I noticed there was someone else tied up in one of the dark corners of the cave. It was White Lily, a young Osage girl, rolled up in her blanket. She's been to a mission school and speaks some English. The Cheyennes hate the Osages and Kaws, ya know, and when they had a fight over some antelope, they captured her and kept her tied up, just like me. I still didn't know who I was then, but havin' someone to talk to made it easier. She was awfully shy and didn't talk much at first. All the Cheyennes did was grunt and point. They untied us only long enough to eat.

"Well, one day I overheard two of the Cheyennes talkin'. I listened close and I heard one of them mention *Charley Bent*. Remember, he was the half-breed son of William Bent who ran Bent's Fort on the Santa Fe into Colorado? When the Cheyenne said the word *Charley*, I felt somethin' tug at my mind, and I hung onto it. I kept on thinkin' about it. Suddenly I remembered I had a brother Charlie, and soon it all came back to me—what my name was, where I lived, everythin'. So then I knew."

He paused and drew a hand wearily over his fuzzy face. "White Lily and me planned our escape. Rather, it was me who planned it because she was too scared to talk much. Remember, we didn't even know where we was. At least, I didn't. Although she thought they had come along the Smoky Hill. I knew there were caves not too far from Ellsworth, so we figured if we could get away we might find our way back to town. But we was watched so close that there was never was a chance to leave, bein' we was tied up. One Injun always stayed to guard while the others left. They came back with meat, so we knew they must'a been out huntin'. Like I said, we was never really treated bad, but she was awful scared. I don't know what they planned to do with me, although White Lily was prob'ly gonna be held as hostage or somethin' from the Osages. They must'a found me after I was knocked out, and took me with them. I never knew what happened to

Queenie. I don't know how long I'd been there, but White Lily said it was 'many moons.' "

"That's what the soldiers at Fort Harker meant about some-one seein' some Cheyenne bucks west of town," Clell said to Charlie. Willie nodded, then continued his story.

"That makes sense. Then one night before the others left, we seen they was drinkin' 'fire water.' After they left, the one who was guardin' us must'a drunk too much and he fell asleep. He got careless and forgot to tie us up after we ate."

Willie grinned. "That's when me and White Lily stole out of the cave. It was pitch dark outside and we couldn't see a thing. We slipped and crawled and slid down a steep hill, and hid in the brush. She had only her blanket to keep her warm. Now and then, the moon came out from behind the clouds, so we crept real quiet along the banks of the Smoky Hill all night to get away from them. When daylight came, we had to keep hidin' so they wouldn't find us. She cried much of the time. She is such a little thing and she was gettin' so tired, but we didn't dare stop. We just pushed ahead. Worst of all, it was so cold we almost froze. Sometimes we heard them close by when they was probably huntin' for us, but we kept real quiet. I told her that God would look out for us and to hang on. She had learned about God at the mission, she said, so we just prayed for Him to take care of us, and He did."

He looked so tired that Barbara wanted to tell him to wait until morning to share the rest, but he draw a deep breath and plunged on.

"We soon realized we was nearin' the Smoky Hill Trail, and maybe we'd catch a ride back to town. But she was shiverin' and cryin' so, that I didn't think she could possibly make it. As I carried her through the bushes along the Trail, we heard a team of horses and a rumble of a wagon. I saw they was freighters so I flagged them down and we got a ride into town. At the depot I thanked them and said we could get home all right. I carried White Lily most of the way. She was so tired and her blanket was so ragged by then that it didn't keep out much cold any more."

"No wonder, she was so cold and exhausted," Barbara whispered. "Now, you march right up to bed, Willie Warren. And sleep as long as you wish. Lily can sleep in the bed in the south room. I'll see that she has plenty of warm covers. Bring a lamp, Charlie."

"Let me hurry up ahead and build a fire in the little stove," Clell offered, scrambling up the stairs with an armload of wood.

Willie staggered toward the stairs, then turned to Barbara with a half smile. "Ya know, you just called her 'Lily.' That's sure a purty name for a nice little girl," he said. "I figured you'd let her stay. Maybe here she won't be so scared."

After Charlie had carried the sleeping Osage girl to the south upstairs room, Barbara came up and tucked her in. Then she shut the door softly and followed Charlie down the stairs.

"Know what, Charlie?" she whispered as she pulled on her nightgown, "I think we should have a praise service before we go to sleep."

"Are you sure you're not too tired? This has been a very stressful day for you." She smiled and shook her head.

After they had prayed, he wrapped his strong arms around her and kissed her.

"Oh, Barbara! This is one of the happiest days we've had at Ellsworth. Maybe things will get better from now on."

Barbara lay awake for a long time. Her heart was as full as Charlie's. Things were bound to be better now, one way or another.

CHAPTER 13

$\mathcal{F}$ebruary weather dawned mild and sunny, and Barbara looked forward to the birth of the new baby in March. Willie had regained his strength and was back at work in the lumberyard.

Like a shadow, White Lily moved quietly as she helped Barbara with the work. She was bright and quick, and so polite, but spoke very little. Yet she seemed willing to learn what she didn't know. She washed the dishes, made beds, scraped vegetables, took on the small chores around the house and entertained the boys.

"White Lily come from Cattail Clan," she told Barbara in a burst of confidence one day. "Osages have much clan, and not afraid to work. Ai, we listen to Non hon Shin Ka, wise men, and they tell us what to do. They learn from Swift Walker, chief of Little Osages. Chief Pa-hus-ka, he head chief of Great Osages. He teach Osages right. And now John Blue Jacket and Red Deer of Cattail Clan lead us."

The boys loved their "Indian sister," as they soon called her, and obeyed her without any fuss.

"A sister helps Momma and loves us all," Danny told Barbara sagely. "I'm glad Uncle Willie bringed her to us."

"So am I," Barbara said. Her body had grown heavy and clumsy and she needed extra time for the housework. Although she had lost much of her tiredness, her back hurt more than ever.

Mame dropped by often after her work at the Old Reliable was done for the afternoon. When Barbara heard a sharp rap on the door and Mame's shrill "Yoo-hoo?" she knew she'd have a guest. Except Mame never considered herself a guest. She immediately set to work with whatever needed to be done.

"You ready for the new young'un, Barb'ra?" was her first comment that afternoon as she helped Barbara fold freshly washed towels. "Have plenty of floor sackin' for diapers? And warm blankets?"

"I saved everything the boys used when they were babies."

"Fiddle-faddle! Stuff wears out. I'll bring some more empty flour sacks from the hotel kitchen and some worn out blankets." She paused. "That Injun gal—Lily, you say her name is? She ain't too much for ya, is she?"

Barbara threw up her hands. "Lily? She's a treasure! Danny and Jem love her. She's a great help, and so quick to learn. In fact, she's out with the boys right now. They're romping in the back yard since the day has warmed up."

"Hmm." Mame tapped a finger against her nose. "More help than my good-for-nothin' niece, I reckon."

"Well—"

"I'm keepin' a tight rein on Nance Drubeck, and she's simmerin' down some. She ain't as feisty as she was once. She also ain't flirtin' with the menfolks like she used to. I guess it must be the Bible she's been readin'."

"Bible?" Barbara was startled. "Do you mean she's reading the Bible Ed Curtis left for her?"

"Glory be, but she's behavin' almost civilized these days. Dunno what you done for her, Barb'ra, but whatever it was, it seems to have worked. She's even kept away from the riffraff downtown. I was afraid she'd want to go back to her old 'job' at that bawdy house, but she seems to be satisfied cleanin' rooms and waitin' on tables."

She laid down the last folded towel and went to the window. "When your little young'un comes, you can lay her in that big clothes basket so she can watch while you're cookin'." Without a word she waddled to the large apple crate that stood in the northwest corner, and tugged it under the west window.

Barbara sighed. *So Mame called the baby "she". No one knows what the sex will be, that's sure. The baby should be in the bedroom where it's quiet,* she thought. *I'll not say anything. Mame means well. That's just her way.*

Before Mame left, she had whipped up a big panful of apple strudel and set it in the oven and added a few sticks of wood to the fire.

"Take it out in 40 minutes. Don't let it get too crusty or it crumbles. Now I must run. Time to fix grub for the hotel. Glad to hear Willie finally got back. I told ya he would, didn't I?" She picked up her shabby coat from its nail and slid her plump arms into the sleeves.

"Yes, you did. But when he came back, I was so surprised, I could hardly believe it. He was gone so long."

"You made 'rangements for help when the young'un comes?'

"It's still three weeks away. We'll work something out."

Mame tied the tattered blue scarf over her skimpy gray topknot and bounced toward the door. "I'd help if I could, but I got my job, ya know." With a wave of her hand, she bobbed out of the house and was gone.

Barbara watched her go. *Mame makes me both mad and glad,* she thought whimsically, *but more glad than mad! I'm glad she came. She wouldn't be Mame Probst if she couldn't "manage" things.*

Barbara decided she'd have to ask one of the farm women to help out when the baby came.

A few days later, just as she had finished the laundry and was wiping up the floor, a knock sounded at the door. Barbara moved ponderously to open the door, and Nance Drubeck stepped inside. Barbara invited her to sit down. The girl had combed her brown hair neatly, and when she took off her coat, Barbara noticed the prim white starched apron over her green print dress. Nance sniffed at the aroma of soap suds that lingered in the kitchen.

"You been washin' clothes, Barbara? I smell soap."

"I'm just wiping up and putting things away. Lily's hanging the clothes on the line right now."

"Lily? Oh, you mean that little Osage who come back with Willie? She knows what to do?"

"She's willing to learn what she doesn't know. She—"

"Guess she ain't like me. I'm s'prised an Indian will work. I thought they was all shiftless and lazy. Besides, she's such a little thing. Can she talk English? Or does she yammer in Osage?"

"She lived on the reservation and attended a mission school, and she has learned to speak some English. Her parents were killed when the Cheyennes fought the Osages on an antelope hunt. That's when they stole her and kept her in the cave where they took Willie. Poor little thing. She was so scared when she came, but now she seems calmed down somewhat."

Nance's green eyes narrowed. "I . . . guess I didn't seem very grateful, Barb'ra, . . . when you gave me a place to stay."

Barbara smiled. "I meant it when I said that I wanted to help you."

"Maybe," she lowered her chin, "maybe I didn't show it, but . . . well, there was somethin' in this house . . . I dunno what it was. I just know you had somethin' I was lookin' for. I—" The frightened rabbit look was back in Nance's face.

"I sensed that, and I tried to show you the love of Christ, Nance. But I'm not sure I succeeded." Barbara expected Nance to snort at her response. Instead she drew a deep breath.

"That's one reason I came over." She paused and drew out Ed's little Bible from her pocket. "I . . . I been readin' this book, even if I said I wouldn't. Didn't make much sense at first, and it still don't. Ya know, that Ed Curtis was always a gentleman—even if every time he opened his mouth, out came a Bible verse. And I got curious what made you folks—and him—so . . . sort of complete, I guess you'd call it. So I been readin' this."

She paused and paged through the Gospels. "It says here,

'For as many as received him, to them gave he the power to become the sons of God, even to them that believe on his name.' What does it mean?"

Barbara drew a deep breath and offered up a silent prayer. "It means that if we receive the gift of God's salvation, we become His children. That anyone who believes on the Savior, the Son of God, can be cleansed from all sin."

"But it can't mean anyone like me." Nance shook her head fiercely. "I . . . I've been a bad gal, and have . . . had a bastard child. There's no way—"

"The verse says 'for as many,' and that means anyone, Nance. Whether they've been good or bad. All you need to do—"

"No, Barb'ra. Not me." She drew her hand over her forehead. "I might as well tell you. I . . . I've fallen in love with Ed Curtis. But that ain't why I'm askin'. I just know he can never love someone like me. He's so good and I'm so bad. It's no use." She shook her head fiercely again.

"Nance, it doesn't make any difference to God. The Bible says 'all have sinned and come short of God's glory.' That means Ed, me, Charlie—everyone. God has taken all our sins away, but we must accept it by faith." Barbara paused. "Nance, even your precious baby—"

Nance jumped to her feet, her green eyes hard. "I don't want to talk about it!" She crossed to the other side of the room, then turned on her heel.

"But I never thought I'd fall in love with someone like Ed Curtis—one whose life is to preach the Gospel. And seein' how I've had a bastard child, he'd never. Still, it's so very hard. . ." Her voice broke, and she hurried out the door without buttoning up her wraps as she fled.

Barbara drew a deep sigh, but a slither of joy swept over her. To think Nance Drubeck was finally interested in God's Word! *I only hope I've been able to help her,* she thought. *Nance must feel very unworthy, insecure, as we all are.* "But Lord," Barbara prayed, "You alone know her heart. If she is really seeking, help her to find You. . ."

February was drawing to a close. The wet snow that had fallen the night before had mantled the house with white and drifted in the shallow draw that led toward the river. As the night grew colder, the icy crust crackled in the wind.

The house was quiet when Barbara awoke in the morning. Had the menfolks already left for work?

As she rolled her heavy body out of bed, she felt that the day would somehow be different from the day before.

When she staggered into the kitchen, Lily stood shivering by the stove. Charlie had let Barbara sleep after he had built a fire, and fixed breakfast before he left the house. There was no sign of Clell and Willie, either. They must've eaten and slipped out quietly. The fire had died down, and the room was cold.

She shook the grate, added more wood to the hot ashes and stirred the faltering blaze.

"You must be cold, Lily," she said.

"White Lily like warm t-t-tepee more better." Her teeth chattered when she spoke.

"I'm sorry. Your room must be cold, too. I should've been up earlier, but somehow—" She sighed. *What's wrong with me?*

"Show White Lily how to make fire."

Bless the girl. She really wants to learn. In a few moments Barbara instructed White Lily in the art of building a fire in the stove.

As the warmth spread through the big kitchen, Barbara stirred up a batch of cornbread. There was a side of bacon in the lean-to, and she cut several generous slices and placed them into the skillet. Lily immediately came to help.

"You warm now?" Barbara asked, and the girl nodded.

Jem toddled into the kitchen, shivering and rubbing his sleep-fogged eyes. Barbara drew him close to her and gave him a hug.

"Lily, could you please bring Jem's shirt and pants? I must dress and feed him. Then you two can eat your breakfast."

The girl left the stove and started for the bedroom when

Barbara let out a startled cry. Lily whirled around.

Barbara placed one hand on her abdomen. *It . . . was too soon. The baby wasn't due until mid-March, almost three weeks away!*

She beckoned to the Osage girl and pointed to the stove. "Please . . . watch the cornbread and bacon, and give the boys some breakfast." Then she staggered to the bedroom. White Lily grabbed Jem and plopped him into his high chair. He began to wail and scream. She patted his head and hurried after Barbara.

"Missy, baby come?" she whispered, her eyes wide and frightened.

Barbara nodded, seating herself on the edge of the bed. "Could you . . . run to get Willie? He'll know what to do. Don't . . . be afraid! Take my coat . . ." A pain knifed through her and she threw herself on the bed. "Danny—" she called raggedly. "Put on your clothes, and give Jem some . . . breakfast. Your Momma's going to have . . . a baby . . ." She sat up and began to unlace her shoes and tried to jerk off her clothes.

"But Momma—"

"Please do as I say, Danny!" Her voice was shrill.

Oh, why didn't I organize all this earlier? she fumed. *I should've told Lily and Willie what to do before this happened and found someone to help. But I thought there was time.* She heard the kitchen door slam. Good! Lily must be running to call Willie.

Jem was screaming in the kitchen while Danny yelled, "Be good, Jem. I'm coming!" He jerked on his trousers and scrambled into the kitchen. She heard the clatter of flatware and tin plates.

Her pains became stronger. She sat on the edge of the bed and clenched her fists. If only she knew of some woman who could help, least of all Nance Drubeck. She knew Mame was busy in the Old Reliable kitchen and Barbara didn't know any other woman in town. She'd never asked the farmer friends from church. *Oh, dear God . . .* She didn't want to frighten the boys, so she bit back her screams. *What was taking Willie so long?*

Pulling on her flannel nightgown, she threw herself on the bed and dug her fingernails into the pillow.

The kitchen door slammed with a gust of cold air. *Thank God, for Willie!* He raced into the bedroom.

"Barbara? Lily said—"

"It's . . . it's the baby . . . early. Go for . . . help. Call Dr. Henson, and hurry! Then go back to your job!"

"But Barbara—"

"Do as I say! There's nothing else you can do. Just hurry!"

"Sure. Don't worry, Barbara. Everythin' will be fine." And he rushed from the room.

Barbara writhed and moaned and tried to shut out all the horrifying thoughts about babies born on the prairies who had died and about women who died in childbirth. She remembered the little Peterson baby and the other infants that had failed to survive at Pawnee Rock. Oh, for Grandma Griffith!

But you have two fine sons, she reminded herself. Both had been born while she and Charlie lived at Cottonwood Crossing. Fortunately tiny Grandma Griffith with her black shoe-button eyes stayed at Lank Moore's ranch when Danny and Jem were born. Aunt Prudy had made sure she was there for Barbara.

But here in Ellsworth she knew almost no one. She'd hoped to make better arrangements. Yet, during the past few months, it had been hard to find the time to do it. With Nance and Clell there, then Ed, she was often busy with housework, and by the time she had a few free moments, it was getting too dark to go outside to visit, so she hadn't really planned for this day.

She placed her hands over her mouth to stifle the shriek that tore at her throat.

Just then she heard voices, then saw the craggy face of Dr. Henson hovering over her. He made a few quick examinations.

"Just calm down, Mrs. Warren," he said in a soothing voice. "You're doin' fine."

Another pain knifed through her and she couldn't hold back the screams. "Charlie! Oh, Charlie, if you were only here to hold my hand!"

Suddenly she felt a rough, plump hand grip her sweaty palm. "Now, don't you fret none, child. Mame's right here. You know you can always count on Mame. If Willie hadn't stopped by the Ol' Reli'ble, I'd have strangled him. Now, push once more. Doc says that's what ya need to do right now. Everythin's gonna be fine. Trust me."

Barbara drew a deep ragged breath, then pushed—hard. Suddenly the awful pain was gone and she felt—free. There was no sound. All was deathly quiet. "Oh, dear God, what's happened to my baby?" she cried. *My baby is dead . . . I've been so tired. Too tired.*

Then she heard a strong, lusty cry, and Mame's grip loosened on her hand.

"Well Barb'ra, looks like you got yourself the girl I promised you. A fine little black-haired thing. Won't the boys be proud? Here, look at her."

Dr. Henson handed the infant, wrapped in a scrap of blanket, to Barbara for a few seconds. The tiny nose and ears and mouth and soft pulsing skull were perfect. The damp hair was long and black, and there were two tiny lines for eyebrows. Barbara drew a deep satisfying breath.

"Not only the boys. Charlie and Willie too. And Lily . . ." She murmured wearily. "Oh, she's beautiful! Thank You, Lord ."

In her preoccupation, she was unaware that the doctor had left. Mame bent over Barbara and pressed her hand once more. "Barbara, you just lay back and rest now. I took off from the hotel kitchen when Willie came, but I gotta finish that pot full of roast beef for the supper. Just go to sleep now. The Osage can look after the boys. I'll tell her. Wish I could stay and take proper care of you and your young'un, but I got my job. I'll come again when I get off work. You made 'rangements about someone helpin' you and the babe?"

Barbara shook her head. "The baby came too early. But I have Lily."

"That Injun gal?" Mame snorted. "What does she know about lookin' after babies? She's just a little thing herself!"

"She's 12, and quick to learn. We . . . we'll manage. After work I'll have Charlie and Willie."

Mame eyed her shrewdly. "Are ya sure? What do menfolks know about such things?"

"Trust me, Mame. We'll get along. Call Lily and the boys to come and see little Sally Ann. I named her for Charlie's mother."

Checking the sleeping infant, Mame *cootchied* with tiny cooing sounds, and hurried to the kitchen. "I'll be back tonight," she called over her shoulder, and Barbara heard the door slam.

Moments later the Osage girl melted shyly into the bedroom, holding tightly to Jem's and Danny's hands.

"Here, boys," Barbara said. She folded back the blanket and uncovered the tiny face. "This is Sally Ann, your baby sister. Isn't she beautiful?"

"She's so little," Danny whispered, cooing gently, while Jem only grunted, "She baby doll."

"She sounds more like a mouse," Danny laughed.

Lily smiled faintly and touched the tiny pink face, then turned to the boys.

"White Lily help with little papoose. You let Missy Momma rest now."

"Yes," Barbara murmured drowsily. "Mame will be back later. Be sure to stoke the fire and look after the boys. I must . . . depend on you, Lily. Can you do it?"

Lily's dark eyes shone. "Ai. White Lily big sister now." And she led the boys from the room. Barbara fell into a deep sleep. Her last thoughts before she closed her tired eyes were of Willie and Charlie and Clell, and the surprise in store for them when they came home.

CHAPTER 14

Spring came early, with warm, quick rains and a sudden frothing of anemones in bloom along the river as the month turned into April. Winter had spent itself, and pale sunlight bathed the drab houses with whiteness, tinting the grasses and prairies with a strange rich green. In the corners of the yard, clumps of wild sweet william poked through the mellow soil, and the air filled with honking of northbound geese.

Barbara, standing at the south window, drew Sally Ann's little blanketed figure close to her breast and smiled. She recalled how proud Charlie was of his daughter, and Willie's tender care in cuddling his niece in his arms. Danny and Jem could hardly take their eyes from her as she lay in the crib Willie had made from scrap lumber. They hung over her when she was awake, and Barbara had to remind them constantly that she wasn't a toy. White Lily frankly adored her. Even Clell took a solemn interest in the baby.

Mame ambled in several times a week, offering unasked-for advice as usual, but Nance seldom came. Perhaps the sight of a tiny baby dredged up painful memories. During one of her rare visits, she confessed she had walked up the street to the bordello door, but hadn't gone inside.

"I decided to get shed of that sort of life," she admitted sheepishly. "It gets one into trouble." Barbara was hopeful about Nance's new attitude toward life.

Now that the weather had warmed and spring had come, Barbara was eager to plant a vegetable garden. The rich black loam in the backyard could yield nourishing fresh food.

With the building boom in Ellsworth, Willie often came home late from delivering lumber, and Clell was kept busy dispensing spring tonics in Seitz's Drugstore. The hills around Ellsworth were black with cattle. With the greatest drive of longhorns from Texas surging in, Charlie seldom came home before dark. The local stockmen and ranchers spent long, tiring hours riding the ranges, making sure the Texas cattle kept to the restricted areas of the Chisholm and Cox Trails and didn't stray into the pastures.

One day Willie came home bursting with news at the supper table. "It seems folks are comin' into town from all directions—Texans, Mexicans, emigrants, homesteaders, stock buyers and drovers. And everyone wants lumber. We can hardly get enough for all the buildings that's goin' up."

"Not to mention the shady bunch: the gamblers, deadbeats, the thieves and gunmen," Clell quipped, spooning more molasses on his flapjacks. "And saloons! They're springin' up in every nook and cranny on the main streets. So many folks are movin' in that the *Reporter* predicts half of Abilene's soon gonna be here!"

"What's the big attraction in Ellsworth all at once?" Barbara asked as she got up to pour more coffee. "The cattle drives? I thought they'd been coming in for months."

Charlie sighed. "Ellsworth city fathers are encouraging the cattle trade. Trouble is, cattlemen think Abilene's getting too lawless, so they want to ship the cattle to the eastern markets from our stockyards. Besides, the drive is shorter from Texas. But with the Kansas governor approving the herd law, the rough element will soon have the run of the town, and that's too bad."

"They already have. Gamblin's really taken off. Them and the saloons is even kept open all night," Clell muttered. "That don't bide no good. A person's almost scared to walk out at night. Talk about Abilene bein' lawless! Ellsworth ain't any better."

"Can't the city keep them out? What about the marshal?" Barbara asked, fear nudging her spine.

Willie shrugged. "Why should they? Our marshals don't have good reputations as it is. And the high licenses the gamblin' places and saloons have to pay are money in the city's pocket."

"So the general public doesn't have much to say," Charlie said with a frown. "Naturally the businesses encourage all this. The extra riffraff trade is good for their cash registers. The stores, especially the saloons and gambling dens, are thriving. Since the herd law isn't enforced, the drovers have the run of the town and the land around it. Or so they seem to think. Of course, we ranchers oppose the herd law's concept of justice. But the marshal and his men look the other way. What can we do?"

Willie reached over and tousled Jem's head. "You boys make sure you stick around home. Some of the newcomers are downright rowdy."

At Sally Ann's persistent cries, Barbara got up from the table and picked up the baby from her crib.

"Here, my precious," she cooed as she nuzzled the soft cheek against her own, "Momma will feed you now." She carried the baby to the bedroom to nurse her. *Was all this true? Were things getting out of hand downtown?* She had tried to send Lily to Beebe's store for things like sugar and coffee when Clell or Willie were busy, but the girl seemed terrified of the rough characters who lounged on the benches in front of Nick Lent's Saloon. The boys had obeyed and stayed close to the house, but what was to prevent the lawless men from roaming the streets?

White Lily was clearing the table when Barbara came back into the kitchen. Darkness had fallen and the yellow cowslip moon swung into the east, scattering white magic over the plains as frogs chirped in the draw. All looked peaceful, yet, in the distance, shouts and yells disturbed the quiet. It wasn't easy to remain calm when a powder keg seemed likely to explode.

After the family had gone to bed, Barbara checked the boys and covered Sally Ann, who whimpered and fretted.

"Lord," she prayed, kneeling beside the bed, "we know a restlessness hangs over the town, but I ask Your blessing upon its people, for there are good people here. Please calm my fears!"

She slept uneasily that night, until daylight edged over the rim of the world. The sky paled and the naked trees along the Trail stood black against the cold gray morning. The gloomy day did nothing to ease her fears.

As she prepared breakfast, Barbara noticed the almost-empty sugar canister.

"You want me get sugar?" Lily grabbed Barbara's arm, her dark eyes frightened.

"No, Lily. I'll go. You stay here with the baby and the boys. I won't be gone long. I also need garden seeds. It's soon time to plant our vegetables."

The fear in Lily's eyes died and Barbara sighed a little. The girl had always been fearful, and going to the small store certainly must frighten her.

Danny immediately ran for his coat. "Can I go with you, Momma? I wanna go outside!"

"Me, too!" Jem yelled, pushing himself in front of Danny.

Barbara shook her head. "Boys, I don't think you should. If you'd stay home with Lily—"

"But we *never* go to the store!" Danny whined. "Please, Momma?"

She drew a deep breath and looked at them. It was true. They almost never got out of the yard except to go to the little church at Thompson's Creek.

"Well, if you promise you'll stay with me, and not scamper off." She turned to White Lily, "We should be back in half an hour. Sally Ann's asleep, and you can peel potatoes and scrape parsnips so they're ready for the stew. All right, boys. Let's get your wraps on. But hurry."

They scrambled into their jackets, and with a wave to White Lily, Danny and Jem headed for the door.

Barbara took their hands as they set out along the muddy path toward town. The stores were a scant two blocks away, and the street bustled with the clatter of wagons, the creak of carts and the hollow thud of horses' hooves.

She drew back her bonnet. The day promised to be warm after all. The clouds had thinned where a thin ribbon of sunshine had widened into a broad band of blue sky.

Most stores that lined the street boasted wooden awnings and board walks. The boys were chatting as they clattered along. Across the streets of Main and Lincoln to the north, the new two-story brick courthouse looked imposing. She knew the new school was being built, and she sighed. Danny was old enough to attend school in the fall, and it scared her to think he'd have to cross the rough, busy plaza on the north side of the tracks.

Just to the left stood Beebe's General Store. Barbara held the door open until the boys had crossed the threshold. It was a pleasant jumbled place, warmed by the big round stove in winter. It smelled of oiled floor boards, new cloth, leather and freshly ground coffee. The dusty front window with a worn green blind hanging drunkenly across it looked out at the rutted treeless street.

Owner Jerome Beebe was weighing out dried beans from a sack behind the counter for a customer. When Barbara and the boys stepped in, his balding gray head and his salt-and-pepper mustache were bent over his work.

"Will that be all, Jake?" he asked as he tied the brown paper sack with a stout piece of string.

"All for now. Martha needs the beans to soak for tomorrow's supper. What's the latest on the Texas cattle trouble?" Jake asked, drawing out his wallet and smoothing out a few crumpled bills.

"All them drunks and drovers and gamblers are really spending their money, and for us business folks, it's good news. Then, of course, there's plenty of loose women . . ."

Barbara drew a startled breath, thinking of Nance.

". . . the sheriff's trying to enforce the law, with the city marshall and four deppities. They're keeping tol'ably good order. You know how the cattle started pouring into the stockyards by the thousands in April. Keeping order while the cowboys must wait ain't easy."

"Yup, the stockyards are addin' on more loadin' pens, I hear," Jake said, picking up his purchases as he headed toward the door.

Barbara had roamed silently about the shop with its musty aromas of dried bean pods and barrels of pickle brine as she picked up scoops of carrot and radish seeds, beans and peas from the seed bins.

Danny spied the glass candy bin. "Looky, Momma! Peppermint candy!" he screeched, and trotted toward the glass case.

"Candy, candy!" Jem shrieked, pounding his chubby fists on the glass.

Barbara hurried after them and pulled them away from the candy counter. "No, boys. Your mother has no extra money for candy. Let's go home."

She quickly opened her purse and drew out the money after Beebe had measured out her sugar and had added up her purchases with a stubby lead pencil. Then he reached into the candy bin for two pieces of peppermint.

"Here, boys. This is my treat."

Before Barbara could protest, the boys had grabbed their candy and promptly gobbled it up. She shook her head and piloted them swiftly out the door. Hitching posts for the teams and cow ponies lined the streets. She glanced to the west where the three-story Drovers Cottage Hotel stood. It had been moved in from Abilene in sections on flat cars.

Several nondescript, bearded, tobacco-stained cowboys lolled on the benches in front of Nick Lent's Saloon. Quickly Barbara rushed by them.

"Let's hurry," she prodded, turning south. "I've left Lily with Sally Ann alone. What if your baby sister is crying?"

Danny looked up at her with imploring eyes. "I should've

saved some of my peppermint for Baby Sister!"

"That's all right." Barbara said with a quick smile. "Sally Ann wants you to eat it yourself, I'm sure."

When they reached the house, White Lily sat in Barbara's chair, gently rocking the baby. The girl seemed to have the lost the frightened look.

"Missy, baby cry and I rock her," she said. "I sing to her— firefly song."

"That's fine, Lily. You did just right."

Barbara laid the sleeping baby in her crib and prepared the stew. After they had eaten and she and Lily had cleared away the dishes, Lily put Jem down for a nap. Danny considered himself too old for naps.

"Momma, I'm seven now. That's gettin' big, isn't it?" he said, thrusting out his chest. "I'll be going to school, you said."

Barbara smiled. "Well, that's true. Then why don't you sit down with one of the books my cousin Bitsy sent? Have you read all of *Black Beauty*?"

"Not all." He shook his tousled head. "Some words I can't figure out."

"I'll help you."

They had just settled down at the table when a knock sounded on the door. Barbara patted her hair and brushed the front of her faded pink skirt and hurried to open it. She seldom had drop-in callers, but today Pastor Levi Sternberg stood there, hat in hand.

"Good afternoon! May I come in?"

"Please do," Barbara said, opening the door. "Here. Take a chair. Have you had your lunch?"

He laughed. "I went to the Old Reliable. Mame Probst said I should stop by and tell you she wouldn't be able to come today. With so many people swarming into town, the hotels are jammed, and she's having to cook for an army!"

"That's what we hear," Barbara said. "Charlie and Willie are afraid things will erupt into a riot one of these days, with all the riffraff in town."

"So far, the sheriff and marshall and their deputies have kept them in line. I hope the problems will simmer down soon. But I wanted to tell you we're going to worship at Larkin's Hall until the new church is finished. Our congregation's growing. Please remember, there's still a handful of strong believers here in Ellsworth."

He called to the boy who was bending over his book. "Danny, we're going to start a Sunday school next week. We want you boys to be sure to come."

After the pastor left, Barbara felt more at ease. If the law was clamping down on the rowdies, and the few churches were growing, surely the Lord would prevail.

That night when Willie came from the lumberyard, he flung his cap in the corner almost angrily.

"What's wrong, Willie?" Barbara asked with alarm.

"Ya know what I read in a newspaper that comes into the front office? It said, 'As we go to press, Hell is in session in Ellsworth.' Now, what does that mean?" His young bearded face grew more agitated.

Yes, what did it mean? Barbara thought, her heart pounding with sudden fear. *Was the disturbance growing worse than they'd thought?*

CHAPTER 15

*B*arbara stepped outside and sniffed the mid-April air. Spring rains had fallen and left the yard muddy. But for the past several days, the shining sun and a brisk spring breeze had dried out the garden plot. Willie had dug up the plot as soon as it was tillable, and it was high time to plant vegetables.

"I'll let Danny and Jem help me sow seeds if you'll look after the baby," she told White Lily. "We should've put the potatoes in last month. Willie always insists they must be planted on St. Patrick's Day, but we missed it. Now's the time. Danny, Jem, where are you?" she called.

Jem dropped his ever-present blocks and shrieked, "Here, Momma."

"What do you want?" Danny said in his most grown-up manner, laying aside his book.

Barbara snatched up her bonnet and held out a pair of straw hats. "Look what Clell brought you. Outdoor hats to keep the sun from your eyes. Let's plant the garden plot Willie raked for us last night. It looks like rain again, so we'd better hurry."

From the trunk she had dug out the old brown alpaca dress that her cousin Aggie had given her last summer with the advice "to wear when you're working with dirt, so the birds will think you're a mulberry tree and come nesting in your hair!" Aggie had always seemed to pick out dark, serviceable yard goods for herself.

Now Barbara pulled the shabby dress over her head and jammed her dark hair under a bonnet. Snatching up the sacks of garden seeds, she held the door open as the boys scrambled outside. Half an hour later the potatoes were in the ground. Then she made long rows with her hoe and let Danny and Jem drop in small handfuls of the vegetable seeds. Jem sprinkled them up and down the row, then scattered the precious peas he clutched in his grimy hands.

"Momma, Jem's not getting the peas where they're s'pose to go!" Danny wailed. "He's spilling them all over. We'll have a terrible garden and it will be all Jem's fault!"

Barbara glanced up at the gray clouds that were scudding across the sky. "Boys, don't fight, please! It's going to rain soon, so let's hurry or we'll get wet."

Ten minutes later big bullet-like raindrops pattered down noisily with a sudden volley of lightning and thunder.

She shooed the boys indoors and hurried back outside to cover the last row of beans with dirt. Before she had replaced the hoe in the shed, another sheet of rain, a flash of lightning, and rolls of thunder pounded from the sky.

As suddenly as it had come up, it was over, and the dazzling blue sky peeped between torn white clouds. Barbara's dress was soaking wet when she came indoors.

"Did we do good, Momma?" Danny said wistfully, his damp chambray shirt clinging to his young figure.

Barbara took off her wet bonnet and hung it on the nail behind the door. "You boys did fine. Where's your hat, Jem?"

Jem pointed to the window. He had stuffed his new straw hat between the open window sill and the pane.

"Wind blow. Make Jem's hat get dry."

Quickly Barbara raised the window pane and snatched it off the window sill. *I only hope it isn't ruined,* she thought. Clell had been so proud when he had presented the hats to the boys. Straw hats were sure to lose their shape if they got wet. All of the window sills on the west side of the house were dotted with raindrops. Apparently White Lily didn't know how to close windows.

Every day, for the next several days, the boys ran to the garden to see if the seeds were sprouting. When the first green shoots pushed through the ground, their excitement knew no bounds.

"Looky!" Jem cried, "Peas come up. See?"

Barbara patted his shoulder. "Yes, that's because you planted them and God makes them grow."

The straw hat, still somewhat damp, had shrunk in size, and tufts of his hair peeped from under the brim. He would turn three in a few weeks.

As the days settled into summer, warm stinging winds swept over the plains and blew piles of fine, sifting soil against the garden fence. The vegetable garden struggled to survive. The peas and beans had been harvested, but the cucumbers and carrots looked pitiful.

All day long, hot winds moaned and crooned over the baking prairie that shimmered in the heat. Barbara was tired long before evening, and the boys fussed and fretted because of the heat. White Lily came and went like a shadow, without her usual cheery nature, her dark eyes troubled.

Charlie came home from the ranch totally exhausted in his sweat-soaked clothes. He often tumbled into bed after a few bites of food. He said that scrawny, hungry cattle stood hunched in the meager shade of the dwindling haystacks or crouched in the sheds, and the roaming Texas cattle bawled for water as they drank up the muddy watering holes.

Sometimes high, cauliflower clouds seemed to hang overhead with the promise of a cooling rain, then dissipated when the incessant wind died at nightfall.

Only Clell and Willie seemed cheerful and plugged away at their work without complaining.

One day a strong wind blew in from the Rocky Mountains with a few black clouds as a brief summer shower sped over the prairie. The air cooled for a few days and spirits lifted.

Yet an undercurrent of uneasiness seemed to permeate the town in spite of the brisk business. During the city election in June, a man named Miller was elected mayor. He won on the platform to maintain strict law and order, and Chauncey Whitney became sheriff. He was believed to be the most decent of the law officers.

Willie said a new theater was being built that could seat 150 persons with a large stage for the performers. A bar stood at the right of the entrance, and a gambling table to the left.

"Another den of iniquity," muttered Clell when he came home from work.

"No wonder Ellsworth is called the liveliest town on the Plains!" Willie quipped. "We're so busy at the lumberyard, we've had to hire extra help. I pray the marshal and his deppities is keepin' order."

Clell cocked his shiny bald head and sniffed. "But the city fathers have done something that could backfire on them! They've actually cut back the number of deputies. I hope that don't spell trouble."

The family sat around the supper table eating bowls of new potatoes with fresh onions swimming in cream. The boys kept a running chatter about the vegetables *they* had planted and were now eating. The day had grown hot again and, even now, the heat hung heavy in the house.

Charlie had grown silent, then he laid down his fork. "It seems everyone is enjoying the prosperity, even if you can almost feel trouble brewing below the surface. They tell me most cases that come before Judge Osborne are drunk and disorderly violations, with Billy Thompson the chief culprit. He's charged frequently with carrying six-shooters and getting drunk. All to no avail. I'm afraid of what that man will do to Ellsworth. He's been arrested, fined and released, time and again."

"Well, as long as he's kept under control—" Willie began.

"I have a theory that he's the person behind all our trouble with the cattle drive. The drovers and cattlemen spend far too much time in the 'dens of iniquity,' as Clell calls them. One of these days all hell will break loose."

"Well, no doubt, the marshal figgers he can manage things,"

things," Willie drawled.

"Just so he keeps it that way. You know, him and his deputies have poor records!" Charlie snorted. "I'm still uneasy."

"Well, the town's boomin' and everyone feels good, so nobody's gonna disturb the waters. You can bet on that," Willie added.

Charlie looked up. "Maybe we should. If we could nip the big trouble in the bud—"

"Better leave matters alone," Clell warned. "What could *you* do?"

"We haven't fenced in our ranges like they did in Abilene to prevent the Texas cattle from moving around freely. So what happens? Thousands of cattle are grazing around Ellsworth, wandering on *our* ranch lands, drinking from *our* water holes, while awaiting shipments to the eastern market. With some fifteen hundred cowboys that have little to do and money jingling in their pockets—added to a town full of gamblers, thieves, harlots, and gunmen—things are apt to explode. Mark my words!" His countenance grew dark.

Abruptly he got up from the table, snatched up his hat and stomped from the house.

Barbara watched Charlie's receding back. She knew he had been under so much stress during the dry summer. And now with the trouble that fermented from the drovers and Texans, he seemed unusually upset.

Already the sun had set and the afterglow deepened to purple. The pink cloud flecks in the east dimmed to misty lavender, and a cool breeze stirred through the open windows.

White Lily had taken the boys outdoors to splash in the water that still lay in puddles in the yard from the last small shower.

Clell went outdoors to sit in the shade on the east side of the house while Willie helped Barbara clear the table. She raised questioning eyes to his.

"Willie?"

"Charlie's really riled up," he said with a shake of his head. "He's prob'ly walkin' off his mad. One can't blame him."

She lit the lamp and set in on the table. "No, you can't. But he's had such a cool head about everything so far that this is hard for me to understand." She picked up the whimpering baby and took off the sweat-soaked little dress, leaving only the diaper. She wiped her skin with a clean washcloth and laid her in her crib.

"Don't worry about my brother, Barbara," Willie said, his voice gentle. "He won't do anythin' rash. I guess he has things he's got to puzzle out."

"You're right, but I hate to see him so upset. And his prediction about the trouble that's brewing doesn't make me feel any better!"

"Just be patient. He'll be back before ya know it."

Just then she heard familiar footsteps and Mame's "yoo-hoo!" at the kitchen door. Willie picked up the water pails and started toward the door. "I'll get the drinkin' water, meanwhile," he said. As he swung through the door with a nod to Mame, she bounced in and found a chair.

"Looks like your family's tryin' to beat the heat," Mame said, wiping a corner of her blue calico apron over her neck. "I seen the boys and the Osage splashin' in the puddles out back."

"Yes, that little shower cooled things down a bit, but we need a good drenching rain."

"This kind of weather tuckers anybody out. How's the young'un?"

"I've already put Sally Ann to bed."

"Poor thing. How she can sleep in this heat is surprisin'! I walked outta that hotel kitchen as soon's the last dish was washed," Mame muttered. "Things is sure ready to pop in town and this heat ain't helpin' any."

Barbara sighed. "It really has Charlie upset. He feels Billy Thompson's behind a lot of the trouble with the cowboys, because they aren't watching their longhorns while they're waiting for more room in the stock pens. They get restless and begin drinking and gambling which the Thompsons encourage. The trains can take only so many head at one time, you know."

"Not only Billy, but his brother Ben, too. Gamblers, both of them. I hear they move from town to town where there's cattle trade and make their gamblin' handy for the cowboys and drovers to get rid of their pay. Lucky they ain't stayin' at the Ol' Reli'ble. The Grand Central's where they hole out. There— or at Brennan's Saloon. Well, I'd better get back. Told Nance I wouldn't stay long."

"How is your niece? She hasn't been here in some time."

Mame struggled slowly to her feet and sighed. "I never would'a believed it. I couldn't do anythin' with her before. Now she's gettin' meek as a kitten. But she's awful restless, too. I don't know what ails her." Mame started toward the door and held it open as Willie lugged in the water pails. "Well, don't get too upset. Things can't get much worse." She slammed out the door and bounced down the walk.

Barbara called the boys in for bed. Their clothes were almost as mud-spattered as their bare legs. Willie set a panful of water on the floor.

"Wash your feet before you go to bed, boys," Barbara said. "Where's Lily?"

"She's still outside where it's cooler," Danny said, jumping into the pan of water with a splash. "She ain't scared as long as Clell's out there."

Clell came in after the boys were in bed. The little man stretched his arms and yawned. "Charlie ain't back yet, is he?"

"No. And I'm getting worried," Barbara said with a sigh, wiping up the wet floor where the boys had been over-zealous in washing their feet.

"Things is gettin' pretty bad downtown, wouldn't you say?"

Barbara nodded, hanging the pan on a nail. "From what Mame Probst said, both the Thompsons are creating disturbances."

"They aren't stayin' where she cooks, are they? I hope she watches out."

"No, they're at the Grand Central, when they don't hang out in Brennan's Saloon."

"Don't worry about Mame," Willie chuckled. "That woman

could fight a runnin' sawmill, if need be."

"Well, it's good of her to stop by so often." Clell stifled another yawn. "I ought to go up to bed, but I'll wait until Charlie gets in."

Barbara glanced at the clock. "It's almost ten. I'm getting worried about him. He's been gone for over two hours."

Clell and Willie glanced at each other. "Let's go find 'em," Clell said, and they hurried out the house.

White Lily had already gone up to bed. Barbara sat in her chair and began to plait her long brown hair. *Dear Lord, please let everything be all right,* she prayed. *Charlie's usually so sensible. Surely he won't stir up trouble! This town's becoming too wild, too rowdy for my family to be safe. With the Thompsons running loose, and gun fights on the street, I'm getting more and more afraid. We've got to move and I don't care where, but somewhere where it's safe.*

As the minutes ticked by, her head was bowed in prayer. Then she heard voices and recognized Charlie's voice with Clell's and Willie's as they came in.

Charlie's face looked haggard and drawn. Tossing his hat on the floor, he threw himself into a chair while Willie and Clell remained standing in the doorway.

"You needn't have sent them after me, Barbara!" Charlie fumed. "I was so fed up with all the trouble the Thompsons are causing with the drovers and cowboys, I went to see Sheriff Whitney. I told him to run them out of town, that Ellsworth doesn't need that kind of riffraff. I talked until I was blue in the face, but he insisted he takes his orders only from the mayor. Well, as long as the cattlemen are here, this town takes in plenty of money, so you can be sure the mayor won't do anything, in spite of his election promise." He shook his head helplessly. "Barbara, I don't know what to do!"

"Couldn't we move away? Isn't there another place for us? The children—"

"What about my job? I don't know where it would be safer. It seems everywhere we go, we think we'll do better. But I've done it again in bringing you and the children to this rough frontier town. Besides, all the newer homes are in just as much danger as we are here."

"But isn't there a farmhouse—someplace in the country where it's quiet, where we could live?" she pleaded. "You could still ride out to work."

He drew a deep breath. "Barbara, my darling, the few farmhouses that are available aren't livable. Some are mere dugouts, lonely and far from any neighbors. I remember how you fought loneliness when we lived at Pawnee Rock and you begged to go where there were people. Well, I don't want you to go through that again. Maybe we'll have to believe Sheriff Whitney when he says he's keeping order, and trust the Lord to keep us. But here you have Mame, and you can at least see our church friends on Sunday . . . and Willie and Clell are close by to keep an eye on you."

He looked so stricken and sorrowful that her heart ached for him. He had wanted to make their lives better, and yet it seemed things were almost worse than before. The Indian menace was over, but now they faced the lawless element in town. Barbara was silent. *What of my family? Dear God,* she prayed again. *What shall we do? Please, God, don't forsake us.*

CHAPTER 16

*W*hen Charlie stormed home from work the next day, the news he brought upset Barbara so much that her hands trembled and she could hardly peel potatoes.

"A vigilante committee's being formed to warn the 'unwanted' to get out of town, or else!" His voice had grown hoarse with anger. "Things have gone far enough."

She laid down her paring knife and came toward him. "Charlie, how do you know so much about all this? You aren't . . . a part of it, are you?" Her voice shook.

"No, I'm not, but my boss Dick Wilcox is. And it's only because I don't want to take part in violence that I'm not!" His hands clenched and unclenched as he spoke. "As a Christian I can't participate in any trouble, but I *am* angry . . . at what they're doing to our town."

"What . . . what do you think the committee will do to make the lawbreakers leave?" she whispered. "Will there be . . . fighting?"

"I don't know what their plans are, since they haven't been finalized. But enough is enough. Even Jesus grew angry with injustice in His day! The marshals have let everything slide and ignored the problem."

The boys rushed into the house just then, screeching and yelling. "We're playing good man and bad man!" Danny

121

shouted. "I'm the good man and Jem's the bad man."

Barbara turned, horrified, to the boys. Her mouth grew dry at this sudden outburst, and she grabbed Danny's shoulders.

"Danny, what do you mean? You can't—"

"Jem's a gambler and lives in a s'loon, but I'm Sheriff Whitney. I gotta make him mind or else he goes to jail. Isn't that the way it's s'pose to be?"

Barbara stood, shaking her head in disbelief. What kind of influence was this wild town having on their sons?

"I'll let you handle that, Charlie," she flared. "But things have come to a pretty pass if our sons are playing out what's happening downtown! Boys, you'd better wash up for supper. We'll eat when Clell and Willie come."

As Clell came in, he gave Charlie a questioning look. "You home already? Usually you ain't in before seven."

"I . . . begged to leave early. In fact, I did want to talk to Wyatt Earp. He's a hide buyer, and I have stretched a few antelope hides he might want to buy. I heard he's here because he's interested in the cattle business. I wonder where I could find him."

"Almost anywhere," Clell chuckled. "He's a good shot, I hear tell, but he looks green as grass. Don't even wear a beard. And he laughs at the way Ellsworth deputies run for cover from the Texans."

"I'll keep him in mind. Tomorrow I'll try to find out what action the vigilante committee has decided to take," Charlie said.

"Legally, they'd best leave the problems to the marshall and the county sheriff," Clell said. "But the law is scared of the Texans, so they ain't much good at all."

Willie came in, looking distraught as he headed for the water pails. "Do I have time to get water before we eat, Barbara?"

"I think so, if you hurry."

He picked up the pails and left without a word. *What was worrying him?* Barbara wondered.

White Lily came in from the bedroom and moved to the

122

stove. She flung her black braids over her shoulders and glanced at Barbara.

"Missy-Baby go to sleep, but she not very sleepy. I sing *Wah-Way-Tay-See*, firefly song."

Barbara smiled. "That was nice. I think she doesn't want to go to sleep because she likes to hear you sing!"

Charlie and Clell sat down at the table as Barbara spooned the fried potatoes into bowls and slid the fried ham onto a platter. White Lily had stripped the first crop of sweet corn, and after Barbara had boiled it, she drizzled freshly churned butter over the roasting ears.

Jem began to bang his fork on his high chair. "Pray, Papa, pray. I'm hungry!"

"As soon as Willie comes, son."

Five minutes later Willie came in with the water. It was more obvious than ever that he was upset.

"Willie? Is anything wrong?" Charlie asked.

"Plenty. There's been another gun fight at Brennan's Saloon," he said quietly. "No one got hurt, but it's the Thompsons again. I seen the whole thing when I helped unload lumber from the freight car this afternoon. John Sterlin' barreled outta the saloon with Billy Thompson on his heels. Billy was totin' his rifle and started shootin' at John, and John took aim at Billy. At first they was just horsin' around, like it was fun. That good-for-nothin' marshal just stood there and gawked. It's gettin' so one feels almost scared to go on the streets."

Charlie and Clell looked at each other. Barbara trembled again. How long would they live in daily fear here in this rough frontier town? As she poured the coffee, her hand shook so much that she spilled some on the table.

She was glad when the boys were in bed and she had persuaded White Lily to go upstairs. *The girl's dark eyes looked frightened,* she thought. *Mine probably do, too. But I must put her at ease. I must remind her that Clell and Willie will be in the other room upstairs, and she is safe.*

For hours Barbara lay tense and awake after she went to

bed. The night dropped a black curtain over the sky as an enormous, orange moon came up slowly hiding behind the clouds. Crickets chirped and a bird stuttered in the darkness. Her mind fretted and scratched in turmoil, as it did whenever she was tense. She prayed for a long time that night, groping for a peace that would not come.

*****

August 15, 1873 started as a quiet day, and the dawn broke sweet and cool. Barbara was pleased at the peacefulness, and she drew a deep satisfying breath. If it weren't so hot, perhaps it might be a good day after all.

After breakfast she and White Lily stripped the husks from ears of corn and cut off the kernels to prepare them for drying. *I wish Mame was here,* she thought. The big, blurry woman always had a better way to suggest, and this time Barbara would welcome it.

The quiet shade on the west side of the house was marred by the scrape-scrape of knives on nubbins of corn. She had shown White Lily how to cut the corn off of the cobs and several pans were quickly filled with the sweet, juicy kernels. The girl learned quickly, as usual, and Barbara wondered, *What would I do without her?*

The boys joined in to help White Lily strip the green husks from the remaining ears while Barbara continued to scrape the cobs. Little Sally Ann lay on a blanket nearby and cooed, her dark blue eyes darting with interest. The morning was already growing hot, and Danny and Jem grew restless. Barbara finally sent them off to play.

Suddenly a volley of shots rang out, and the sound of yelling and shouting echoed from downtown. Figures were running from the rear of several stores a scant two blocks to the north. The boys rushed toward her, screaming with fear. Barbara scurried to meet them and flung her arms around them both.

"Get into the house—quick!" she ordered. They whirled away, and seconds later she heard the kitchen door slam.

Then she hurried toward White Lily, who crouched, terrified, beside the pans of corn.

"Lily, you take the baby, and I'll bring in the corn but be careful. Don't fall!"

The girl, still frozen with fear, staggered to her feet mechanically until Barbara snatched Sally Ann from her blanket and thrust her into White Lily's arms.

"Now, go!" she snapped. Then she picked up the panfuls of cut corn and headed after her into the house.

Jem huddled in one corner, crying, while Danny sat at the table stoically, his face drawn and tense as Barbara locked the front door.

Jem's sobbing had changed into a long, slow whimper. No one spoke. It was as though everyone was numb with horror and fear, sitting motionless—all but Sally Ann, who gurgled contentedly on White Lily's lap.

I must do something, Barbara thought. *Lord, what can I do but pray?* The words bobbed shakily from her lips. " 'Thou wilt keep him in perfect peace whose mind is stayed on thee.' That . . . that's what Jesus wants us to . . . to do."

After the gunfire had died, there was a frantic pounding at the door. "Open up! It's me—Clell!"

Woodenly, Barbara moved to the door and unlocked it. Clell's short, grim figure stumbled inside, his bald head bobbing.

"I . . . wanted to make sure . . . you're all right," he panted as he stood in the middle of the kitchen.

"What going on?" Barbara whispered anxiously. "Where's Willie?"

"He's comin', so don't worry. I'll tell you . . . what happened," he continued as he tried to catch his breath. "Please sit down."

Unsteadily, Barbara moved toward White Lily, picked up the cooing baby and took a chair. The Osage girl crouched, ashen-faced, in the corner.

Clell squatted on the floor and drew a deep breath. "It all started with a poker game in Brennan's Saloon. It seemed the stakes was unusually high. Ben and Billy Thompson began to heckle and force the play, with Billy drinkin' real heavy. Soon there was an uproar. Billy and Ben rushed to get their guns, shoutin' threats from in front of the saloon. Wyatt Earp, loungin' on the bench in front of Beebe's Store, watched the whole thing. Then Sheriff Whitney appeared to check on the trouble. It seems John Sterlin' slapped Billy's face. Billy got nasty and mad and hit John on his mouth. That's when John and Billy got into a real fracas."

He paused and drew his hand over his bald head. Barbara sat frozen at Clell's words. Danny and Jem still shivered at the table.

"Go on," Barbara whispered through tight lips. "What happened then?"

"That was the yellin' you heard, I guess. Then Billy invited John to get his gun and meet him outside. John hit him again and knocked him down. Billy and Ben dove for their guns. Then Sheriff Whitney, without carryin' a weapon himself, tried to talk to John Sterlin', but John's friends hurried him out the back door. The sheriff faced the Thompsons again and invited them in for a drink. When he come out, he told Wyatt Earp that Ben and Billy had finally quieted down."

Clell drew a deep breath and swallowed just as the door burst open and Willie barreled in. His young face looked strained and agitated.

"Then Billy staggered out with Ben's shotgun and fired at Whitney three times, hittin' him in the chest and arm," Clell went on. "He fell, all covered with blood."

"Yup, I saw it too. That's when a couple hundred Texans swarmed into the plaza south of the tracks," Willie put in. "These gun-totin' Texans was mostly friends of the Thompsons. When Ben and Billy headed across the tracks, the Texans stormed after them. Not a single Ellsworth marshal was in sight! Billy jumped on his horse, a-cussin' and invitin' a fight, but found no takers, so he rode outta town real slow. I saw it all."

"But where was the marshal? The deputies?" Barbara gasped. "Surely someone—"

"Remember, they *thought* they had things under control, so they kept outta sight. Willie, you stay here with Barbara while I go check on what's happenin' now."

"Be careful—" Barbara began, but the round little man had already scurried out of the house. "What's going to happen now, Willie?" she gasped.

Willie shrugged his shoulders. "We'll have to wait and see. All's quiet now."

Just then Charlie rode up. His horse was flecked with foam from the furious ride into town.

"Barbara! Danny, Jem—are you all right?" he shouted as he stormed into the house. "We heard shots as we were driving a few head toward town, and I came to see if you were safe. What's going on, Willie?"

In a few words, Willie told Charlie what had happened. Without a word, Charlie sprang to his feet and left.

"Charlie!" Barbara screamed. "Please come back . . ." But she knew he wouldn't be satisfied until he was sure his family was out of danger.

Willie glanced at the clock. "You got somethin' to eat, Barbara? I'm hungry."

"Hungry!" Barbara snapped. "At a time like this, who can eat?"

"Well, things has calmed down now, so we'd better spoon down some vittles."

Slowly Barbara scooped some corn kernels into a pan and pushed it on the stove to cook. She sliced thick slabs of wheat bread and set out glasses of milk. Then she told the boys to come to the table. Jem gulped down his milk down while Danny picked restlessly at his bowl of corn. White Lily sat in her corner and refused to move. Willie had wolfed down his meal in a hurry. A numbness seemed to permeate the room.

An hour dragged by, and Willie returned to work. When there was no sign of Charlie and Clell, Barbara grew anxious. To pass the long minutes, she took her time about washing the dishes and tidying up the kitchen. She covered the pans of corn with some clean tea towels, hoping the corn wouldn't spoil before they spread it on the shed roof to dry. Then she put Jem and the baby down for their naps. White Lily sat down at the table and stared out the window as though deep in thought. Danny paged restlessly through *Black Beauty*.

When Charlie returned some time later, he sank into a chair and sighed. "It looks like the trouble's over. At least, for now," he muttered.

"What . . . what happened? What did you do?"

"Me? Nothing. I wanted to see what was happening."

"Happening?" Barbara gave a shrill laugh. "Happening, when we were frantic with worry—"

"Well, it seems Billy had ridden out of town, but Ben was still around. Meanwhile the marshal's deputies were arming themselves. But since Sheriff Whitney was badly wounded, there was no one to give orders. The deputies finally decided to take the violators dead or alive, just as Mayor Miller came along. Because no arrests had been made, he fired them all, leaving no one to make arrests!"

"Miller," Charlie said, "shouted across the plaza to Ben Thompson, but he was met with profanity and jeers and whoops of laughter. They were in an ugly mood and the town was in a very tight situation.

"Then Wyatt Earp made a passing remark to the mayor about his so-called law and order, adding that it wasn't any of his business, but if it were, he'd arrest Thompson, or kill him. Mayor Miller angrily snatched the badge from one deputy's shirt and gave it to Earp. 'I'll make it your business!' the mayor snapped. 'You're now the marshal of Ellsworth. I order you to arrest Ben Thompson!' Earp swaggered across the street toward Thompson. The Texans were already backing away from Ben, as Earp slowly started toward him, because they'd heard about Earp's fast gun. Earp calmly told Ben he'd rather talk than fight. 'I'll get you either way, Ben,' Earp told him. 'Throw down your gun and raise your hands!' And that's exactly what Ben Thompson did. He was arrested and fined $25. The charge? Disturbing the peace!" Charlie snorted. "Twenty-five measly dollars for all the trouble he caused in town! What a laugh!"

Barbara gasped, letting out her breath slowly. "What we need is a marshal like Earp."

"Oh, the mayor offered Earp the job, but Earp declined. I guess for the Texans the fun was over. They all dispersed and everything's quiet once more."

Barbara looked at Charlie. "I guess we never were in real danger, were we?"

"Not from the bunch downtown. Let's pray that with the Thompsons gone, the Texans will settle down. Sheriff Whitney is in bad shape though. He needs our prayers."

He paused dramatically. "Barbara, I don't want to put you through that again. I'm going to try to find us another, more quiet place to live."

Barbara stood on tiptoes and threw her arms around his neck. "Oh, Charlie, the sooner the better!"

CHAPTER 17

$\mathcal{T}$he days dragged by, hot and windy, and spirits sank. Six days later the vigilante committee was ready to act. Sheriff Whitney had died a few days earlier from gunshot wounds, and consternation ran high. The townspeople were angry. They ordered a posse to look for Billy Thompson, but he had slipped through their fingers. Tensions mounted.

"I don't think they was lookin' very hard," Willie grunted. He sat on the floor, playing with Jem and the carved horse.

Barbara moved like a manikin as she cooked and tried to keep calm. "But isn't it great that the marshals finally stood up to the Texans?" she ventured as she served the beef hash and settled the boys at the table.

Willie shrugged. "We'll see."

"Well, it's about time!" she fumed.

Sheriff Whitney's death had outraged the citizens. Charlie said the vigilantes now insisted that a "white affidavit" be handed to the "unwanted," with orders to get out of town in 24 hours—or else.

"Believe it or not," Clell chuckled, "Ben Thompson skedaddled before he got his!" He pushed his palm over his shiny forehead. "And some of the others is gettin' mighty edgy."

Yet things were far from settled. This latest conversation sent a chill down Barbara's spine, and Charlie's table grace was most fervent.

"But if the Thompsons are gone—" Barbara began, scooping beef and vegetables into Jem's bowl.

"We still have the Texans to contend with," Charlie said gravely. "Not all of them are bad, of course. Some are law abiding, but they've all had about enough of this mess. The troublemakers are the ones to watch. Now they're threatening to burn the town because they've been ordered out of Ellsworth."

"Do . . . do you believe they'll do it?" Barbara sputtered.

"It won't happen, if the vigilantes can help it. I know some are preparing to fight."

"What'll they do next?" Willie asked, spreading butter on his bread. "I hear some of the law-abidin' Texans are plannin' to leave their cattle at Wichita, now that the Santa Fe railroad has reached there. It would save them a heap of time, since it's some 70 or more miles closer to Texas."

Charlie and Clell looked at each other, and Charlie lowered his chin. "Well, with the drought, it would get them away from here. The worst of it is, cattle prices are already dropping. I'm afraid Ellsworth is in for a bad time."

"What about your job, Charlie?" Barbara said as she got up and reached for the coffee pot.

He shook his head. "I know Wilcox is deep in debt, and so are many other ranchers. We may have to pull out our stock and start over on a spread somewhere else. It's getting critical. I'm looking everywhere for another place right now."

The worry was still with Barbara the next afternoon when Pastor Sternberg was at the door. He doffed his gray hat and fanned himself as Barbara invited him in and pulled out a chair. The hot winds blew through the open window and the thin checkered curtains dallied, batting the warm air into the kitchen.

"I wondered how you folks were getting along with all the trouble that's been brewing here."

Barbara picked up the fussy baby and jiggled her on her hip. "It's not been easy. When we moved here we had such hopes for a fresh start," she sighed. "But it seems trouble follows us wherever we go."

"The Lord never promised the Christian life would be easy," he said. "But He did promise He would never leave us nor forsake us. The work on the new church is continuing. But with the drought and the cattle prices droppin', it may come to a halt. I have another bit of news for you, Barbara. I may be able to help the Osage girl get back with her people."

"Shall I have her come in to talk with you?" asked Barbara.

"If you would, please."

When White Lily came into the room, a shy smile lit her face as she saw the pastor. She walked toward him and offered her hand, and he shook it warmly.

"Would you like to go back to your tribe?" he asked kindly.

"*Ai*! I want much to go." She glanced anxiously at Barbara. "But she need me to help with Missy-Baby."

"Lily," Barbara said quietly, "You have been a great help, but if you can go back to your people, please go!"

"I'd like to get word to your tribe, but I must ask you more questions," Pastor Sternberg said. "Why not come and stay with us for a few days?"

With a nod, Barbara went upstairs and packed the Osage girl's meager wardrobe into a clean flour sack. Then she hugged her gently and said, "Come back whenever you're ready. You can stay with us as long as you like, you know."

Barbara watched them drive away in Pastor Sternberg's buggy, with White Lily's dark head bobbing beside the gray, felt-hatted pastor.

Mame bounced in the next afternoon, and her florid face was flushed from the heat. "Ain't seen you since all the fightin' downtown. Figured you'd be goin' to pieces with all them rumors floatin' around. Where's the boys?"

Barbara sighed audibly. "Playing in the back yard. Mame, what kind of rumors?" she asked. "As if we don't have enough to worry about," she murmured under her breath.

"Blasted heat!" Mame fanned herself with her big floppy straw and shook her head. Then she picked up the baby and tickled her chin. "She crawlin' yet? My she's lookin' right pert."

"Oh, she's starting to scoot around when we put her on the floor," Barbara said, folding the stack of clean diapers. "If only we could get out of this town before the rough Texans cause any more trouble. Poor White Lily! She's terrified. I've sent her along with Pastor Sternberg for a few days. They live where things are quieter, and he's going to check on getting her back with her people."

Mame bounced Sally Ann up and down on her plump knees and the baby shrieked with laughter. "Well, guess that's best for now," she said. "She oughta go back to the Osage mission."

"I know. That's what Pastor Sternberg is working on. Although she's been a great help to me."

"Prob'ly more than Nance was when she stayed here!" Mame snorted.

"How is your niece? I haven't seen her in quite awhile."

Mame shrugged her plump shoulders and set Sally Ann on the floor. "She's awful quiet. Not that brash, sassy-mouthed gal she used to be. Don't know what's botherin' her, though. If I don't miss my guess, I'd say she's moonin' for that missionary you had stayin' here last winter."

"Missionary? Oh, you mean Ed Curtis!" Barbara gasped; then she smiled a little. "She took care of him, you know. And I couldn't believe how she began to calm down during those weeks. But one thing she couldn't stand was for him to quote Bible verses. Still, she kept the Bible he left for her, even though she threatened to leave it behind."

"And she's been readin' it ever since. Well, now I'm worried that she's plannin' to leave. I don't think she's forgotten what that soljer did to her. You know they're figgerin' on closin' Fort Harker with the Injuns calmed down now." Mame paused. "But what about you? Things is not lookin' good for Ellsworth, since them Texans threatened to burn the town. Them's the rumors I was talkin' about. What'll you do next, Barb'ra?"

Barbara knew that buyers for the cattle had become fewer

because of crop failures, and financial reverses had wiped out banks in the East and already paralyzed businesses in Kansas. Cattlemen, like Dick Wilcox, were unable to borrow money and threw more and more cattle into the open market, demoralizing the cattle industry. Great numbers of cattle were put into winter quarters on the dried grass around Ellsworth to wait. They were gobbling up what little feed there was left.

She got up and moved the baby away from the open door. "Charlie's looking for a place for us to live, out of town somewhere. I know I'll be lonely, but maybe safer, too. And we must find another ranch!"

"Hmmm. Sounds smart to me. Tell you what. With all sorts of men gaffin' and spoutin' off at the hotel, I pick up lots of news. I'll keep my ears open. You know I'll let you know what I hear."

I'm sure you will, Barbara thought with a wry smile.

*****

Since the Texas cattlemen had begun to leave their herds south at the Santa Fe stockyards in Wichita, the gamblers and saloon keepers were growing restless about the drop in business.

Ellsworth would long remember August 21, 1873 as the day the roughs and gamblers began their exodus out of town. Their threat to burn the town had fizzled out as the townspeople armed themselves and patrolled the streets, ready to put out any fires. A pitched battle was apparently too much for the gamblers and ruffians to consider.

As things quieted down throughout the next several days, the outlook grew a bit brighter. For the first time in weeks, Barbara began to breathe easier, although the heat and drought continued unabated. The pastures and cupped valleys to the west lay toasting under the hot sun, while grasses and row crops shriveled.

It took every ounce of strength Barbara possessed to keep

the house tidy and the baby cool. White Lily was still at the Sternbergs'. The boys seemed to attract grime and dust by merely looking at it, and Barbara despaired of keeping them clean. The heat, the stress and turmoil of the past weeks had dragged her down, and she felt like a drifting shadow.

When Willie came home from work one day in mid-September, he wiped the dust from his neck and flopped on the floor for a moment, fanning himself with a wadded-up newspaper.

"The cropland's been dried out and grassland's been trampled to dust by too many cattle," he said with a sigh. "The streets are filled with a cloud of dust so thick you can't even see a cigar danglin' in front of a man's face. It wears a person out just unloadin' a load of lumber in this heat."

Clell, who was washing his face at the wash basin, grunted, "Folks is gettin' edgy. With more Texans movin' out, at least the dens of iniquity will have to close down, too. That's one good thing comin' out of all this."

Just then Charlie came in, his dusty face creased into a wide grin. He sailed his hat into the far corner of the room and grabbed Barbara's shoulders. "Darling, I've found it!"

"Found what?" She tossed the inevitable wet washrag on the table.

"Our place. Three miles north of town. A rancher who thought he was riding high suddenly went dead broke. It seems someone with money here in Ellsworth bought it up and is looking for a respectable rancher to lease it! The house, my darling, is a two-story limestone. It has a fireplace in nearly every room, and a water pump in the kitchen! It's not a plantation, but it's as close to one as you'll find here on the Plains. We're moving as soon as I can round up our cattle and clean up the place."

Barbara moved back and stood with her mouth open. "Please don't joke, Charlie Warren! This is no time—"

"It's no joke, Barbara. The new owner stopped me as I rode into town. It seems he's had his eye on me for some time. It pays to be 'respectable', my love!"

"But how will we make it? The dry pastures—"

"Oh, sure, we'll have to deal with that, but much of the grass is bottomland and well-watered. I can always work on the railroad for extra cash. What do you say?"

She leaned herself weakly against the table and drew a deep breath. *With all the bad news that had plagued them for weeks,* she thought, *surely there must be catch.*

Charlie's face clouded. "I haven't wanted to tell you until I knew for sure, but my boss warned me weeks ago. I learned he just lost his ranch. It seems the New York Stock Exchange has closed its doors, and panic is sweeping the financial world."

Barbara found herself growing limp. *No! How were they going to survive?*

Fear not . . . for I have redeemed thee, I have called thee by thy name; thou art mine. When thou passest through the waters, I will be with thee; and through the rivers, they shall not overflow thee: when thou walkest through the fire thou shalt not be burned; neither shall the flame kindle upon thee. For I am the Lord thy God, the Holy One of Israel, thy Savior.

The words from Isaiah seemed to flow through her, and a sudden peace overwhelmed her.

CHAPTER 18

*E*very day the September sun blazed from an overhead oven. Outside, the wind crooned and mourned along the river among the scant grove of cottonwoods that hung heavily, as if exhausted.

Barbara stood in the doorway, holding the wriggly Sally Ann, who tried to push away the little pink bonnet that Barbara had tied under her dimpled chin.

Charlie brought the rig up before the house. This was the day they were to drive out to see the new place. White Lily was still at the Sternbergs' while the pastor was trying to locate her tribe.

Danny and Jem noisily hopped onto the rear of the wagon, yelling and shoving.

"I wanna sit right here!" Jem wailed, and Danny gave him a cuff that sent him rolling to the edge.

"Boys!" Charlie called out sharply as he helped Barbara to the wagon. "That's enough! Either you behave or I'll find me a switch!"

"But I didn't do anything!" Jem cried. "Danny's just . . . mean!"

Danny turned his face away. "I . . . I guess I feel sort of mixed up when it's so hot. I'm sorry."

Barbara drew a deep breath. She knew the searing heat and

choking dust made everyone edgy. The wind gusted. The immeasurable, everlasting Kansas wind had given the state its name. The wind had dried out the croplands that were already trampled by too many hungry cattle. Stinging bites of dirt whipped through the air and dusted the blue sky with gray, as the rig rolled out of town and followed a hilly trail to the north.

Barbara closed her eyes tightly against the dust that swept across the fields. It hardly mattered anymore that they were moving to the country, away from the frontier town that had created so much havoc in their lives. She thought once the trouble with the Texans was over, things would settle down and life would return to normal. But the drought and the heat, not to mention the collapse of the cattle market, had continued to plague them from every direction.

Charlie clucked to the team and turned to Barbara, who sat in silence beside him, rocking the baby gently in her arms.

"You're in deep thought, my darling. What's wrong?" he prodded gently.

She continued to sit quietly for a few minutes as though she hadn't heard him. Then she opened her mouth. "Charlie, when will this awful drought, this terrible heat end? And what will we finally do out here? We thought we were going to better ourselves at Ellsworth. Then the trouble with the cattlemen, the collapse of the market—"

"I don't know, Barbara," he said dejectedly. "I was *so sure* things were going to get better. Believe me, I never thought it would come to this, that we . . . that I'd lose my job with Wilcox. I'm so thankful for our small herd, and if we can hang on and things get better—"

"That's all I ever hear, 'when things get better'!" she flung out bitterly. "But, so far, everything's gotten worse."

Charlie didn't answer. The boys in the rear of the wagon chattered and yelled at gray bunnies hopping over the ditch and meadowlarks warbling from fence posts.

Finally he spoke. "My precious Barbara, I didn't *know* things would happen as they did. If I had—" He paused.

"If you had, what then?"

"I don't know. But I still feel the Lord's in this somehow. Rains will come again. They always do. The skies won't be brass forever. Remember what it says in Genesis: 'While the earth remaineth, seedtime and harvest, and cold and heat, and summer and winter, and day and night shall not cease.' If we can just hang on . . . I'll get a job on the railroad—" Suddenly he pointed. "Look! There it is. I think you'll like it."

The tall, two-story limestone house rose majestically in a mounting of young elms and plum bushes at the end of the lane, and Barbara caught her breath. There were wide porches, sturdy brick chimneys, and quaint cornices over the high windows. She almost expected magnolia bushes beside the drive! Charlie was right. It was about as close to a plantation house as she'd ever seen on the Kansas plains. It was magnificent!

"I . . . but Charlie . . . who?" she sputtered.

"It belonged to a rancher who lost it in the crash, as I said. One of the business people in Ellsworth bought it as an investment. It was Mame Probst who told the new owner about me. The man will lease the place to us, and with careful managing, I think we can do it. You'll be away from the tensions of the town, and the boys will have plenty of room to stretch. I feel we're blessed at getting a chance at this."

He pulled the rig to a stop and the boys jumped off immediately. Charlie helped Barbara and the baby down and then led the way through a rusty iron gate and onto the stone porch. The house was dusty, but the rooms were spacious and airy, and there was a quaint charm about the dark wainscoting, the high windows and ceilings. She stood in the doorway of the large front room, unable to speak.

"A-coo?" gurgled Sally Ann in Charlie's arms as she reached out to Barbara.

"Yes, darling. How do you like our new home?" Barbara said, picking her up and nuzzling her cheek against the moist neck. "I think it's . . . very nice, don't you, Baby?"

"I thought you'd like it," Charlie said with a pleased grin.

"We'll get moved in by the end of next week," he said, stepping into the kitchen. "And look what you have here. A pump with a good well right beside the house. No more being stingy with water, and right above the sink, too. And see those cupboards, and that pantry? It all needs a good scrubbing, of course, but maybe White Lily can help?"

"She may leave soon, you know. Pastor Sternberg may have found her tribe."

"Yes, he told me he'd written to Mahlon Stubbs at the Kaw Mission."

"Mr. Stubbs? Oh, yes, I remember him. He was an Indian agent who assisted at Council Grove." Barbara opened the doors of the roomy cupboards in the pleasant kitchen as she talked. "Now, if only we can stock the pantry with food! It means Willie will ride out to town every day to work, I suppose," she added.

"What of Clell Dobbs?" Charlie asked. "I doubt that he'll move out here with us."

"Do you realize for the first time in our married life, Charlie, we'll have all the room we need?" She grinned saucily. "I . . . I'm sorry for being so short with you on the way over here, but I had no idea—"

"As I said, it's about as close to a plantation home as you'll ever have, my darling."

Jem and Danny had scrambled up and down the stairs, yelling with sheer delight. Barbara still couldn't believe this place, although she had seen a few brick and limestone houses spring up in Ellsworth.

After Barbara had seen the rest of the house, Charlie turned to her. "We'd better drive back to town. I have many errands to run. And Willie and I must make plans to move our herds as soon as we can, since I no longer work on the ranch." He picked up the wide-eyed baby and called to the boys. "It seems they're quite taken with the place," he added with a grin.

"Oh, Charlie, so am I! But who is the new owner?" she paused in the doorway and looked at him.

He drummed his fingers on the doorjamb. "You probably

don't know the man, Barbara. But Cady Benson bought it from the Fultons—"

"Cady Benson! Isn't he a gambler?" she jerked her head stiffly. "Charlie, are you telling me we're going to rent it from—*that* man? How could you?"

"What do you know about Cady Benson that I don't know? It was Mame Probst—"

"What does Mame have to do with this? Or with him?" she flared.

Charlie shrugged and started for the wagon. "I don't know, but she told me he was reliable. He'd made a mint of money off the Texans with his gambling business, and he decided to invest some of it. If Mame vouches for him, shouldn't we be satisfied?"

"What if he'll do us in, Charlie, and we lose our herds—everything we have?" she said in a defeated voice.

"I don't think it will happen. He may have been a big gambler once, but if he's Mame's friend, don't you think we should trust him?"

Barbara was silent on the way back to town. For one brief hour she'd been blissfully happy with the prospect of a fine home and pleasant surroundings; then to learn that Cady Benson was to be their new landlord. A bitter taste filled her mouth at the very thought. Sally Ann fretted and nuzzled her damp face sleepily against Barbara's shoulder.

Charlie spoke little until they reached their ugly gray house south of the tracks. Then he drew a deep breath.

"Barbara, I'm sorry if I've offended you, but if you'll talk to Mame, you might change your mind."

"Believe me, I will!" she spat out. She'd been pushed almost too far today, and she didn't know how much more she could take.

Once back in the house, Barbara placed the baby in her crib, drew off her bonnet, then washed her face in a basin of tepid water. *How luxurious to have all the water they'd need . . .* Then she pushed the thought away. The idea of the gambler as their landlord still rankled her. She fanned herself with a folded newspaper as sweat trickled down her arms.

Charlie had taken the boys with him as he left on his errands, and she lay down on the bed to rest. Everything seemed to push her down and she couldn't help herself. She felt as though the whole world was pressing on her chest with a heaviness she couldn't push away.

Lord, I don't understand it. Just when things begin to brighten, everything goes gray again.

She heard a knock on the door and the familiar, "Yoo-hoo? It's me—Mame!"

Before Barbara had pulled herself off the bed, Mame had bounced into the house.

"Barbara? You sick? Charlie said you needed me!"

Barbara came into the kitchen and pulled out a chair for the big blurry woman who stood in the middle of the room. "Oh, Mame, I'm glad you're here. But—"

"Now, what're you frettin' and stewin' about? I hear tell Charlie's found this . . . this really nice ranch out north of town, but you ain't happy with the arrangement. What's the problem?"

"It's the landlord. Cady Benson—"

"Is that all that's worryin' you? Because he run a gamblin' joint once? Barbara Warren, let me tell you somethin'. I know Cady Benson's been a hard man, but since he's been stayin' at the Ol' Reli'ble, I've gotten to know him. Barbara, he's sold his business and plans to go back East. Fact is, he's even been listenin' to me talkin' about the Lord. He—"

"You mean, he's no longer a gambler?" Barbara asked.

"Not no more, he ain't." She lowered her voice a bit, "Fact is, he's been beggin' me to marry him, but I ain't promised. Still, he wanted to leave his propitty in good hands. So I told him there wasn't no better rancher than Charlie Warren."

"About your marrying him, Mame. What is all this?"

Mame kicked off her clumsy shoes and wiggled her bare toes. "I . . . well, I married Henry Probst, hopin' he'd come to the Lord someday, but he never did. I don't want to make that mistake again."

"And you think," Barbara fumbled for the right words, "that Cady Benson wouldn't give us a problem if we moved on his place?"

"I know he wouldn't. Fact is, he was the person what borried the Fultons the money for the ranch. So when they couldn't make it, he just took it back. Said Fulton never did know how to ranch. Cady ain't a rancher nor a farmer, but he'd like to leave it in good hands. He's got considerable holdin's in Boston, and says it's time he goes back there."

A feeling of weakness came over Barbara. *This was stunning news! If it were so—*

"You . . . always know what to do, Mame," she faltered. "And I trust you. Th . . . thanks for what you did for . . . for Charlie, for us." Tears sprang into Barbara's eyes and cut shiny paths down her hot cheeks.

"Just hesh up, Barbara," Mame sniffed. "Let me know when you need help to clean up that place. I'll be down to help you. You know that. If I can show you where to put your things—"

Before Mame had finished, Barbara heard the rattle of a buggy and the snorting of horses. She hurried to the door just as Pastor Sternberg helped White Lily down.

"I brought your little girl back," he called in a jovial voice. "She'll be with you another week or so. You'll be pleased to know that we've located her tribe."

"I help with Missy-Baby," White Lily said softly, her dark eyes full of shadows. "Soon John Blue Jacket come with my Osages to take me with them."

Barbara raised questioning eyes to the pastor. He nodded and smiled. "That's right. As you know, the Osages have been badly dealt with. When they had to leave their reservation in southeast Kansas because of drought and grasshoppers, they roamed over the state. They ran into a band of marauding Cheyennes who kept them from hunting antelope, and they got into a fight. They probably wanted to keep her as a hostage.

"I asked her many questions. She said the Cheyennes left her strictly alone in the cave, except for giving her food. I've

143

encouraged her to try to put this experience behind her. I know what you did for her, by taking her in and giving her love and making her part of your family. This has already helped to heal wounds."

"But where has the tribe been in the meantime?"

"They were driven by hunger to steal cattle from the Texans who were on their way to our stockyards, and soldiers caught up with them. The government is moving them to the reservation in Oklahoma. I thank God you took her in and gave her a home when she needed it. It was with Mahlon Stubbs' help that we found them."

Barbara laid a gentle arm on White Lily's shoulder. "Of course, you'll stay with us as long as you need. But we know you want to be back with your people."

The wind had died down and a sweetness seemed to shift over the late afternoon like the scent of coming autumn.

Mame got up as she shoved her clumsy shoes back on her broad feet. "It's time I get back to the Ol' Reli'ble kitchen and whip up vittles for the evenin' meal." She reached out her hand. "Goodbye, Pastor Sternberg. Make sure there's plenty of paper fans in church next Sunday so folks can push the heat around when you preach." Then with a quick whirl, she scudded out of the kitchen door and was gone.

Barbara told the pastor about the news of their pending move to the Benson ranch. He smiled when he noticed Barbara's enthusiasm about the place.

The day, so full of tattered emotions, had waned, but somehow a sort of peace filled Barbara's heart. White Lily and Barbara quietly stepped outside with the pastor. He swung up to the buggy seat and gathered the reins in his hands. He looked at Barbara and shared a Bible verse with her in parting.

"Thank God, He still lives," she breathed reverently, and Pastor Sternberg lifted his right hand and agreed fervently, "Praise His Holy Name!"

CHAPTER 19

$\mathcal{T}$he next week Barbara packed for the move and began cleaning the new house with White Lily's help. They scrubbed the large, airy rooms in the mornings, before the heat became overbearing. Mame also helped with the cleaning whenever she could get away from her job. No room was quite finished until Mame pronounced it clean. Rattling up the long, dusty lane on a rented horse, her bulky figure swayed into focus from the blurry hot September landscape. The sight of her coming astride the horse reminded Barbara of that first month after they moved into their sod house in 1866. Mame would come clattering up on her old mule, ladened with food—and advice.

The convenience of the pump in the kitchen seemed luxurious, since the job of carrying pails of soapy water up and down the stairs to clean the rooms seemed to be unending. But gradually all the dust and cobwebs were cleared away from the fine rooms.

Every day seemed as dry as the day before. The heat radiated from the vacant sky, relentlessly baking the prairies into giant slabs of toasted vegetation. Mercifully, their well continued to yield a fresh supply of water, in spite of the drought.

The boys had explored every nook and cranny of the ranch and soon discovered special hideaways: the hayloft, the small bluff of layered rock north of the house, and the clump of wild plum bushes that crouched beside the lane. Barbara took comfort in the promise of shade from a row of young elm trees that had been planted in front of the house.

Sally Ann always seemed to be underfoot as she crawled around on the floors of the empty rooms. Barbara grew impatient with the interruptions from the infant's constant whining presence.

"Missy-Baby she not want to play on dirty floor," Lily said, picking up the baby. "She want to go home."

Barbara squeezed out the last rag and hung it over the kitchen doorknob. The baby had whimpered and fretted all morning, and Barbara was worn out.

"I know. It's time we start back to town anyway. No wonder she's so fretful. It's been so hot, and we've neglected her frightfully." She paused and looked at the clean, gleaming kitchen windows. "Wonder where the boys are? I'll hitch up the team and we'll head back to Ellsworth. Everything's clean and shining now. I can hardly wait to move in! You can bring the baby while I round up the boys."

She picked up her old sunbonnet and tied it securely over her dark hair, and headed for the door.

"Boys," she called out, "time to go home. I think we're all finished. As soon as your father and Uncle Willie get our stock moved here, we'll be ready to bring the rest of our things. Danny, can you help me carry the scrub buckets?"

Jem had already scrambled over the wagon wheel and scrunched down to look out the back. As soon as White Lily and Sally Ann were settled amid the pails, boxes and baskets, Barbara clucked to the team, and the wheels creaked down the dusty lane toward town.

When they reached the tall, ugly gray house, Barbara took Sally Ann while White Lily and the boys climbed to the ground and ran off to play on the shady side of the house. Clell had stopped by for lunch and offered to take the team to the barn.

The baby seemed flushed and hot, and the tiny face screwed into a pucker. Barbara almost gasped at the feverish glaze in the usually bright eyes. A soft little moan escaped from the baby's dry lips. A gush of stool oozed from the diapers, and Barbara grabbed for a fresh one from the bag. Diarrhea! She hurried inside.

Just as she finished changing the baby, she heard the rattle of a buggy and went to the kitchen door. Pastor Sternberg pulled the two-seater to a stop. Barbara immediately saw the two black-haired, solemn-faced Osages with him. Their red tunics were tied with leather thongs around their waists. They sprang from the front seat and stood beside the buggy.

"White Lily's people have come," the pastor said. "They're ready to take her to the reservation in Indian Territory. They want to leave tonight while it's cool."

His words jolted Barbara, although she knew that this moment had been drawing near. White Lily's quiet presence had become a part of their family, and her absence would not be easy on Barbara.

"Oh ," she paused. "I think she just went into the house. I'll call her."

Laying Sally Ann over her shoulder, Barbara hurried inside. Now that the time was here to say goodbye to the Indian girl, a wave of sadness swept over her.

"Lily?" she called softly, "your people are here." The girl whirled around and her dark eyes widened. No doubt she had become attached to the Warren family through the past months. *It won't be easy for her to leave us either,* Barbara thought.

White Lily followed Barbara outside. As she saw the two Osages, she ran forward eagerly and grabbed their hands in hers. Then a chatter of Osage dialect followed with motioning and short, guttural grunts.

"Barbara, this is John Blue Jacket and Red Horse," the pastor said as he motioned toward each of them. "They are good people and I know they'll treat her well. Thank God you took her in and loved and cared for her these past months. I know it meant much to her."

"She helped make our world brighter, too," Barbara said in

a teary voice.

"We go now," White Lily said quietly. "I get my things," she added, and scurried into the house. Barbara patted Sally Ann's back gently as she waited. *I'll miss Lily more than I ever dreamed possible,* she thought. *What a help she's been!*

The girl came out of the kitchen, swinging her flour sack with her skimpy belongings in her left hand. With her right, she touched Barbara's arm.

"I will miss little Missy-Baby, and, and you all. Willie —" her eyes grew moist. "If he not bring me here . . ."

"We'll all miss you, Lily," Barbara said softly, squeezing the brown arm. "But go with your people. They love you and they'll care for you. I'll tell Willie you said goodbye. Remember that God loves you, and He'll never leave you!" Barbara tried to choke back the tears. The boys appeared from around the side of the house and White Lily turned to each of them to say goodbye. They each hugged her and watched as she turned away.

Pastor Sternberg took White Lily's elbow and helped her into the buggy. The two Indians nodded and climbed in after her. Barbara watched the buggy move down the dusty street.

The baby had grown very quiet, and the crisp black curls lay damp against her cheeks. As Barbara carried her into the house, she became alarmed at how hot and pink Sally Ann's cheeks had become.

For the next few hours Barbara held the sick child almost constantly while the boys played quietly in the corner. She tried to cool the feverish brow with a damp washcloth, but Sally Ann seemed to object. Charlie and Willie had come back from driving their small heard of cattle to the new ranch and began to clean out the sheds.

Could the baby have the illness called "summer complaint"? Barbara wondered anxiously.

Clell offered to get any medicine that they needed from the drugstore. "I'll ride out to the pastures for some fennel," he said. "Fennel's an old Injun remedy for summer complaint."

Willie had come inside and overheard Clell's remark. "No,

let me do it," he offered quickly. "Make sure there's plenty of water to keep the baby cool," he called out as he left.

Clell picked up the buckets and followed him out.

When Charlie came in, he soaked scraps of old toweling in water and laid them on the baby's hot forehead while Barbara rocked her gently and crooned.

"I wish I'd learned Lily's firefly song," she muttered to herself, pushing the long damp hair from the tiny face. "It always seemed to soothe Sally Ann."

Danny had tiptoed toward Barbara. "I think I know it. It goes: Wah-wah-tay-see, little firefly," he began rather boisterously. At the baby's screams, Barbara shook her head.

"Please, she wants it very quiet now. Boys, please go outside and play."

"But Momma," Jem wailed, "it's too hot outside! Me wanna be in here with you and Sally Ann."

"Yeah," Danny muttered. "We sure need Lily now."

Barbara looked up and frowned. "Danny, why don't you look after Jem? You're a big brother." Danny took Jem's hand and they went outdoors.

Barbara reached for another clean diaper. The pile of soiled ones grew larger. When Charlie came in he stroked the soft silky hair; then he picked up her limp little hand. It fell like a rag when he let it drop.

He stared anxiously at Barbara. "What if it's the paralysis?" He paused and drew a ragged sigh.

"Oh, no!" Barbara gasped.

"That's what the Lingenfelder baby had."

"Was she . . . like this?"

"No, not exactly . . . not really. From what Fred told me, she had a fever and was fretful for a few days. And then she got like this. But she couldn't move."

"She died."

"Yes, the next day."

They stared helplessly at each other for a movement. "Oh, Charlie, please go get the doctor—quick! We must make sure—"

Charlie grabbed his hat and was gone.

Barbara stroked the tiny fingers and wept. *Surely Sally Ann didn't have the dreaded paralysis!* "Dear God," she whispered, "please . . . please let our precious baby get well."

Clell came in with the water pails and paused in the bedroom doorway. "How is she?"

Barbara shook her head stonily. "Not good. Charlie's gone after Dr. Henson."

Then she looked at Clell. "Have you been aware of anyone having . . . the paralysis . . . around here?"

Clell scratched his bald head and deliberated. "Cain't say for sure. But it's a sneaky sickness. It hits children so often when it's hot like this. Is there anythin' I can do, ma'am? I'll do whatever I can. You know that."

She raised her stricken eyes. "Could, could you give the boys something to eat? They must be hungry. I had to send them outside."

"Sure. I'll fry some bacon and fix eggs. Are there plenty?"

"I don't know, Clell. Fix whatever you can find."

Just then the kitchen door slammed, and Charlie and Dr. Henson hurried in. Swiftly the doctor took the baby in his capable arms, checking reflexes as he pressed and probed with practiced fingers.

Barbara hovered over him, feeling numb and crushed. She looked into Charlie's face. He seemed so weary, so tired. The burden of moving, and now this. . . . He came toward her and placed his arms around her. Then he touched the doctor's shoulder.

"Is it the paralysis?" he choked out.

The doctor looked up. "I can't be sure. Her reflexes are quite normal, but sometimes it takes awhile until the limbs show any signs of weakening. There's been a large outbreak of cholera at the Fort, but I doubt this is it."

He handed the baby back to Barbara and drew a bottle of liquid from his bag. "Here. Let's try this remedy. If we can stop the diarrhea, perhaps there's hope."

Just then the slam of the door and the familiar, "Yoo-hoo?"

announced Mame Probst's arrival. "What's goin' on here?" she blustered as she pushed Charlie aside and elbowed the doctor away. "Willie stopped by for a minute to tell me. I came as soon as I could get away."

Barbara raised her stricken face to the big, blurry woman. "The . . . the baby's very sick. We were afraid it might be the paralysis—"

"Here, let me hold her." Mame snatched the whimpering child from Barbara's arms and touched the tiny hot cheeks with plump, gentle fingers.

Dr. Henson had gone to the kitchen for a spoon. "Give her a teaspoon of this every two hours," he said when he returned. "See if you can get her to swallow it. And give her plenty of good nourishing food if she can keep it down. Then we'll wait and see." Grabbing his bag, he headed for the door, and Charlie saw him out.

Wait and see! The words sounded cruel and unreal. Mame was crooning and rocking the baby gently, touching the puckered face tenderly.

"If only I had some sassafras, I'd fix her some tea," she said brusquely. "I've nursed many a babe in my day, Barbara, and this looks to me like the 'complaint.' It's my guess she'll turn the corner by mornin'. Meanwhile, you grab some vittles and keep your spirits up."

"But I can't eat! My baby's so sick—"

"Fiddle-faddle! Now git!"

Willie came in, his arms loaded with crisp stalks of dried fennel. He stepped to Barbara's side and touched her arm. "How is she now?"

Barbara shook her head. "She's still very sick. We . . . we don't know, but it's possible it is the paralysis."

He drew back sharply and whirled around. "I'm gonna go out to Pastor Sternberg's 'n round up a prayer meetin'. Don't forget. God's powerful and He's still in charge."

After he had left, Barbara leaned over Mame who still cuddled the baby in her arms. Mame's crooning continued. Then, with one bold look, she said, "Didn't I tell you to get somethin' to eat? And while you're in the kitchen, boil some of that fennel into a tea. Later, we'll feed it to the baby. Give me another clean diaper will you?"

Slowly, Barbara took a fresh diaper from the rapidly dwindling pile on the shelf and left the room.

I'm not hungry, Barbara told herself, *but I need some food . . . and rest.*

Somehow the long, weary evening waned and a cool wind blew through the open window. Barbara could see the dark arches of the low hills that flanked the Smoky Hill River, and the cottonwood trunks that reared white and gaunt above the banks in the moonlight.

After she had eaten a square of corn pone and cleared away the crumbs of the eggs that had dried in the greasy skillet, she washed her face in a basin of cool water and poured the fennel into a glass jar. The spicy aroma of the tea drifted through the kitchen.

Clell had insisted the boys sleep upstairs, and Charlie had put them to bed. Then he came to stand behind her quietly.

"How is our baby?" he whispered, placing his strong arms around her.

"Asleep, I hope," Barbara said in a low voice. "Let's go see."

He took her arm and they walked into the bedroom. Mame was still hunched in the shabby rocker. In the lamplight she fanned the baby with a folded newspaper. She looked up as Barbara and Charlie came in.

"Shhh," she hissed softly. "She's a-sleepin' now. Sort of a shallow sleep. And her face ain't so hot. If you get the fennel tea fixed, we'll see if she can swaller a bit of it when she wakes up."

"Let me get it," Charlie said, and hurried into the kitchen for the baby bottle. When Sally Ann whimpered, Mame raised her up a bit and held the bottle to the baby's dry, cracked lips, while clucking and urging her to sip. With a small gasp, Sally Ann began to suck, and Mame looked up with a knowing smile.

"I think she's turnin' the corner. Now you lay down and get

some rest, Barb'ra. I'll hold her. Charlie, you go sleep upstairs with the boys, but see that Barb'ra rests. In the mornin', I'll send Nance over to help look after things."

Without a word Barbara drew off her shoes and lay down on the bed, still in her sweat-stained blue gingham.

I mustn't fall asleep, she told herself firmly. *Still, with Mame there, I can relax for just a few minutes. I never realized I was so tired.*

Daylight came, slow and gloomy, and Barbara sat up quickly. She hadn't heard Charlie come downstairs. How long had she been asleep? She looked up to see Mame's bulky figure slumped in the rocker, still holding Sally Ann, her eyes closed.

Jumping to her feet, Barbara pattered toward the chair. "Oh, Mame, I-didn't mean to fall asleep—"

"You was plumb tuckered out, and you needed the rest. Now I'll let you take your babe while I stretch my legs. I've got a dozen crimps in every joint!" she chuckled. "But—your young'un's gonna be fine. She's been sleepin' natural all night."

Struggling to her feet, Mame laid the sleeping infant in Barbara's arms. Barbara noticed that the flush of fever over Sally Ann's face had softened to a soft pink in her cheeks, and a sudden weight lifted from Barbara's heart.

"Just as I figured. The complaint. It wore itself out, and I'm sure the fennel helped."

Barbara looked up sharply. "Then it wasn't the paralysis or cholera at all? We were so worried."

"Doc Henson never treated anyone with the p'ralysis in his life, I wager. I seen right away it was nothin' but the complaint." Mame's tart tone of voice made her view of his diagnosis quite clear. "It was the fennel. That, and Willie's prayer meetin' was what done the job, I guess. Now I'd better hurry back to the Ol' Reli'ble and rustle up some grub for the roomers for breakfast."

"But you never got any rest," Barbara yawned.

Mame stooped over, planted a wet kiss on Sally Ann's forehead, and bounced out of the house without an answer.

Barbara called a sleepy "thank you" to Mame, but it echoed in the dim stillness of the early morning.

When Charlie and the boys stormed in demanding breakfast, Barbara was praying with gratitude to God for helping them through this latest crisis. They paused for a moment and waited until she raised her head and smiled.

Willie had appeared at the open doorway and grinned. "I hope ya didn't mind that I stayed at the Sternbergs all night. Pastor and I really rattled heaven's gates with our petitions," he said sheepishly.

"I got to say g'bye to White Lily, too. The Osage party took out last night. She seemed real happy to go, but said to 'tell Missy Barb'ra that she had a peek of God's heaven in this house these past many moons.' She'll never forget what you did for her."

Barbara's eyes misted. "Neither will we forget White Lily!"

She laid Sally Ann into her crib and checked to make sure she was sleeping normally. The diarrhea had stopped, and Barbara knew there was a vast pile of soiled diapers to wash. How she longed for the pump in the kitchen of the new place to make it easier!

Charlie was loading the wagon with things they were to move. He would soon head out to check on the cattle in the corrals at the ranch. Willie left shortly for the lumberyard.

As Barbara came into the kitchen, Jem rushed toward her and hugged her legs. "Momma, Baby Sister better now?"

"I think so," she said as she smiled down at him. "But please be very quiet so she can sleep. I'll fix a stack of flapjacks for breakfast. Why don't you and Danny go with your father after you've eaten?"

She nudged him toward the table. *How will I ever be able to finish all the work that's piled up while we've been getting the new house ready?* she thought. *Mending, laundry and cleaning up this place . . . If White Lily were here . . .*

But she was glad the Osage girl had found her family at last.

As soon as Sally Ann had perked up, they would move into the big house.

Clell had told her earlier, he would stay in town near his job after they moved, although Willie opted to ride back and forth from the ranch to his job.

"I'll get a room at the Ol' Reliable and stick my feet under Mame's table to sample her cookin'," Clell said with a shy grin. "I guess she's about the best cook in Ellsworth County, so you needn't worry about me not eatin' good."

"Clell, you'll be in good hands." Barbara said, flipping another flapjack. "You'll never know what a great help you've been," she added.

Clell cleaned up the last bite of food and then carried his plate to the dishpan. "It was a pleasure, ma'am," he said as he headed toward the door.

CHAPTER 20

Suddenly he was back. He set his valise down against the wall and sniffed the air. The aroma of flapjacks sizzling on the griddle sent tantalizing fragrances into the kitchen.

"I won't mind havin' a few more of these patty-cakes, even without sausagers," he said. Barbara looked up from her cooking and smiled as he picked up a clean fork and pulled his chair up to the table for the second time that morning. He stabbed three flapjacks from the steaming stack on the serving platter and continued between bites, "There're still some cattle left which haven't been shipped out. No market for 'em out East, so beef's real cheap. Some folks are even killin' the cattle for tallow. "

Charlie said, "There's more money that way than in the meat. Or lettin' them die."

"Shall I get more water for you before I go to work?" Clell turned to Barbara.

"Oh, Clell, would you? I have loads of diapers to wash. If you could help out a bit longer—"

"No problem." After he washed his hands at the basin, he took the buckets from the corner, then slammed out of the house. A few moments later, Charlie and the boys had cleaned their plates and left for the ranch.

At Sally Ann's cry from her crib, Barbara hurried to the

bedroom and picked up the baby and held her close.

"Oh, my little Precious!" she whispered. "Your cry is such a hungry cry. It's time for your breakfast."

Soon Clell came in with the pails of water and set them down. "Anythin' else, ma'am?"

"No, not now. Thank you, Clell!" she called from the bedroom.

"I'll check back with you each day until you're all moved in at your new place. Maybe you'll need more water or somethin'." Then she heard him leave.

As she carried the baby into the kitchen and prepared a thin gruel, Barbara heard a knock at the door. Nance Drubeck stood uncertainly on the stone step.

"Come in, Nance!" she called. "I'm feeding the baby right now."

Nance walked into the kitchen with a poise and charm Barbara had never noticed before. Her brown hair shone like mahogany and was twisted into an attractive roll at the nape of her neck. Her neat, pink gingham dress fell from the fitted bodice into a full, gathered skirt. The white ruching around the neckline set off her fragile coloring, and Barbara thought to herself, *Why, Nance Drubeck is looking beautiful!*

She pushed out a chair with one hand and motioned the girl toward it. "My, this is a lovely surprise. I haven't seen you in quite some time."

"No." Nance sat down slowly and shook her head. "I guess I ain't —haven't—been out in awhile. I was in church last Sunday, but you wasn't there. Aunt Mame said you might be needin' my help today. How is your . . . baby?"

Barbara stroked Sally Ann's silky hair. "Thank God, she's much better. Let's chat awhile, before we tackle that pile of wash."

Nance sat down and began, "I was hopin' to ask you about a few things." She paused. "I . . . I'm plannin' to leave Ellsworth, though I ain't decided exactly where to go."

"But why do you want to leave? And what would you do?" Barbara prodded gently. "Do you have a job prospect?"

Nance shook her head. "I've been waitressin' and cleanin' rooms at the Ol' Reli'ble." She sighed. "But it's just time I go."

"But why go, Nance? What's your reason?"

"I might as well tell you, Barbara. I . . . had a letter from Ed . . . Ed Curtis. He plans to stop here on his was back to Oregon in a week or so. But I can't see him."

"Why not? I thought you liked him. And your aunt said you were reading the Bible he left for you."

"That's just it! Barbara . . . I accepted Jesus Christ as my Savior about a week ago—"

"Oh, Nance, that's wonderful!"

"Now life ain't—isn't—the same. You know what I was when you came here. And I . . . I know I love Ed Curtis, but there's no way —" Her voice trailed away.

"No way, what, Nance?"

"There's no way I can see him, knowin' I can never be . . . There isn't anything left for me here."

"But why isn't there? You've given up your old life and you have a job here. I'm sure Ed would be most happy to hear—"

"Barbara, you know," Nance cut in, "you know what kind of a person I've been—and the baby and all. And if Ed knew that?" She didn't finish the question, but leaned forward toward Barbara and said, "It's somethin' I haven't wanted to talk about, you know. But . . . please tell me about my . . . my baby, Barbara. Now I want to know."

Barbara shifted Sally Ann to her shoulder and smiled, for the baby had just cooed softly. "Your baby was beautiful, Nance. She had thick dark hair, and a little sort of butterfly mouth. She was absolutely perfect!"

Tears sprang into Nance's green eyes and ran down her cheeks. "Oh, God, why did I have to lose her? All I could think of was . . . how I got with child . . . and that I was a prostitute and didn't deserve her!"

"But God loves you in spite of your past, Nance. Now that you've committed your life to Christ, you can start over. Don't you know that?"

Nance clasped her hands on her ginghamed knees. "That's

why I must leave. Yes, I want to start over. But all this . . . this bein' a Christian is so new to me. Barbara, where is my . . . my baby buried?"

"Ask Pastor Sternberg to show you. He and Clell conducted a little burial service for her, committing her body to the earth and her soul to Jesus."

Tears spilled from the green eyes once more. "That . . . that was so good of them. When I see your baby, Barbara, I could cry my eyes out, now that I realize what I lost!"

"Don't forget that the Bible says, 'The Lord giveth and the Lord taketh away. Blessed be the name of the Lord.' And Jesus said, 'Suffer the little children to come to me . . .' Oh, Nance, let the Lord help you carry your burden. You've repented, and He wants to be your Friend!"

For a long minute Nance sat quietly watching Barbara feed Sally Ann. Then she got up and walked toward the pile of dirty diapers in the basket by the window.

"Let's get started now. That's why I came today. To help you. Thank you for all you've done for me. I'll never forget you."

"Let me put the baby in her crib and I'll get the soap and water ready." Barbara paused as she started for the bedroom. "You really plan to leave if you've no place to go?"

Nance shrugged her thin shoulders. "Somewhere . . . there'll be a place. As soon as I know for sure. I'll take the train out of town."

With a feeling of sadness, Barbara laid Sally Ann in her crib. *I'll miss Nance Drubeck,* she thought. *I understand how she feels about leaving, but I wish she'd stay. Dear Lord, please guide her in this decision.*

CHAPTER 21

September's thin, faded skies had finally yielded to the deep blue of October. The wind still blew dust in tangled skeins between the stones of the front walk. North of the big limestone house, the dried stalks of corn rustled their long, brown fingers eerily, as if beckoning with low, sibilant voices. Loose black soil that had whipped in the strong gale lay banked up against the rail fences and barns.

The family had moved into the ranch house two weeks before. Sally Ann was round and rosy with good health again, and she crawled all over the wooden floors of the large airy rooms that Barbara worked hard to keep neat and tidy. Their home life seemed to center around the spacious kitchen in the limestone, as it did in most houses. Charlie and Willie planned to build a few new furnishings for the parlor and the bedrooms in the new place.

The boys never seemed to tire of exploring the wide open spaces of the farm, but when the wood box was empty, they were nowhere to be found.

To earn money for the family's needs, Charlie had taken a job on the Kansas Pacific Railroad as a section hand. Willie rode into town daily to work at the lumberyard, and was beginning to pick up some carpentry skills through his work. Clell had settled in at the Old Reliable Hotel to be near his work at the drugstore.

According to Mame, who trotted to the ranch on a rented horse as often as possible, Clell had made himself useful at the hotel whenever necessary. The druggist's work at Seitz's was somewhat sporadic, and sometimes he talked of leaving for a large city.

"He's such a handy man!" Mame said, rocking sleepy Sally Ann in her ample lap. "If he sees a shingle flappin' or a loose shutter bangin', he gets his hammer and nails and fixes things right there. Such a good-hearted man I never seen before. If he wasn't such a runty thing, I'd take a real shine to him. He needs a good woman," she sighed. "But as long as Cady Benson's hangin' around, I don't hanker for another admirer."

"Mame!" Barbara burst out. "You said yourself Cady wasn't a believer, so why do you even look at him?"

The big woman eased herself out of her chair, laid Sally Ann in her crib and leaned against the doorjamb.

"Oh, I ain't really hankerin' to get married, but when I think of fixin' vittles for other folks for the rest of my days, I get sort of fidgety. And as long as I can keep Cady in line, it's to your benefit, you know."

Barbara sighed audibly. "Nance hasn't left, has she?"

"Not yet. The gal's so mixed up she don't know Adam from Eve."

Then she waddled to the door and looked out. "Looks like maybe we could get some rain. There's clouds hangin' black against the west. I better go before it pours."

For weeks people had nurtured hopes of a good downpour. It was hard to believe that a year ago they'd had a wet, cool fall. Barbara stood outside, staring at the darkening horizon. A cow suddenly appeared on one of the swales of grass, stopped, then trotted away and disappeared in the draw. It was probably a stray from the cattle drive.

She frowned. Now with their own cattle to feed, they didn't welcome the strays that gobbled up scarce fodder. The broken stalks of dried corn had helped their feed problem, but they certainly didn't need stray stock to forage whatever was left.

Buyers were few because of crop failures and financial reverses had begun to paralyze business all over Kansas. She knew that cattlemen, unable to borrow money, had thrown more and more cattle onto the open market, breaking the price even more. Since many longhorns had been put into winter quarters on the meager grass around Ellsworth, they roamed everywhere.

The thousands that were being killed for the tallow instead of meat helped the railroad trade.

Barbara was thankful for Charlie's job, even if his paychecks were modest.

She called out to the boys, "It's time to feed the hens and bring in stove wood."

Then she went back into the kitchen to prepare the evening meal. They had plenty of beef to eat these days because it was so cheap. A hearty stew swimming with generous chunks of carrots and turnips bubbled on the stove. She mashed a large bowlful of squash and dotted it with fresh butter from the cellar, then sliced thick slabs of fresh-baked bread.

The air from the open windows had cooled considerably, and she shut them against the early evening.

The boys had finished the chores and brought in a basketful of chips. Willie worked hard almost every evening after he came home, chopping up tree branches that had grown brittle in the dry winds. They needed every bit of stove wood they could find.

Charlie and Willie, in the ell off the kitchen, were washing up at the gray enameled basin. Charlie dried his hands on the roller towel and came into the kitchen.

"Good thing Shanghai Pierce was persuaded to keep bringing his herds to Ellsworth, even though most Texans are shipping herds from Wichita now, since the Santa Fe railroad has reached there." He paused to pick up a gurgling Sally Ann. "Guess who came in on the train today, Barbara?" he added.

"Someone I should know?" she asked, dipping the stew into a large blue bowl and setting it on the table.

Charlie grinned. "Ed Curtis, on his way back to Oregon. He

headed for the Old Reliable to take a room—and to see one pretty waitress, if I don't miss my guess."

"So he did come. I'm glad Nance Drubeck didn't leave after all," she said, raising one eyebrow. "She said she didn't want to see him, but she couldn't go until she'd found another job."

"Maybe the Lord's kept her here until such a time as this," Charlie said, clucking to his wide-eyed baby daughter who squealed with laughter. "What do you think will happen now?"

"I really don't know. She confessed to me several weeks ago that she loves him, but feels she's not worthy of him." Barbara paused. "Come on, everybody. Supper's on the table."

As Jem and Danny scrambled into the kitchen, Willie pulled out his chair and sighed. "You don't know how good it is not to lug in all that drinkin' water!"

"Oh, I believe you!" Barbara paused and peered out the window. "Do you think it will rain?"

He thumped his lanky body into a kitchen chair. "I doubt it. We've waited so long—"

"And we can wait some more—if we have to," Charlie cut in. "All right, boys. Let's pray."

Barbara pressed her lips into a thin white line. For days they'd been sure that the rains would come, but each day had dawned with brassy, sun-filled skies.

*****

Danny's schooling had become a concern recently. She hadn't spent much time teaching him over the summer, so she dug out whatever books she could find after the move and started reviewing in hopes of sending him to the new school a mile to the north upon its completion. After she had put the baby down for a nap and settled Jem with his toys, she sat down with the seven-year-old and opened the books. Danny was an apt pupil, but today he fussed and fretted.

That afternoon when a buggy clattered onto the yard, Barbara was glad to close "school." It wasn't often that company stopped by for a visit. She pushed back her dark ringlets and patted her bun as she went to the door.

Nance Drubeck let herself in, and after a quick hug for Barbara, she eyed Danny sharply. "He's a-studyin'?"

"Yes. We can't let him neglect his education, so we're doing the job at home. But right now, he's glad for an excuse to stop!"

Danny waited for Barbara to give him a nod to exit the table stacked with books.

"Wish I'd had some schooling. I might'a taught school. I learned to read, but that's about all." Nance shrugged her thin shoulders as she ran her hand over the cover of *Webster's Dictionary*.

Dropping into a chair, she laid her head on the table and sighed. Then she looked up. *Her green eyes look deeply troubled,* Barbara thought.

"Barbara, all I've ever done was come to you with my troubles. But you said once, you wanted to . . . to help."

"And I still want to help. What is your problem today, Nance?"

"Barbara . . . he . . . Ed came by yesterday."

Pulling out a chair, Barbara sat down and faced her. "So you didn't get away after all."

"I didn't know where to go!" Nance burst out. "And as long as I keep my job at the hotel, I have money comin' in. But," she pulled at her fingernails. "He . . . Barbara, he wants to marry me! And—"

"And what, Nance?"

"There ain't no way that can happen. You know I ain't—am not—worth gettin' hitched to a decent man like Ed Curtis! But he won't leave me alone. He keeps insistin'—"

"Does he know of your commitment to Christ?"

"Oh, yes, I told him! And he said he was sure it would happen if I read the Bible he left behind. But—"

"But what?"

"You know about my background. All about my . . . my baby . . . and . . . and the life I lived before. There's no way under the sun that I can marry a missionary. I should've disappeared long ago when I first realized I was in love with him."

"Nance—"

"He calls me *Nancy*. Can you believe it? Sounds so classy and respectable."

"I've often wondered why you ever chose to become a prostitute, Nance. Or if you really did choose it. Sometimes I feel you didn't really—"

"You're right, Barbara. I guess I was sort'a led into it. My Ma was Aunt Mame's younger sister, you know. And my Pa, well, he was . . . trash. Ma died when I was seven. My Pa, bein' so rough, he took me along to all the crummy roomin' houses while he gambled and drank. He . . . before long, he . . . began to abuse me. I hated it and I hated him. I grew up in those places and I felt kinda trapped. Where could I go? I was forced to be . . . ya know, a prostitute to get by.

"Aunt Mame blames my Ma for my fallin' into prostitution. But she didn't know about all the things that was happenin' after Ma died. She wanted me to come live with her and Uncle Henry, but Pa wouldn't hear of it. After Pa died in a brawl when I was 16, I didn't know what else to do. So I . . . I kept on with this lousy job 'cause it paid good. But deep down, I . . . I always wished I could get out. And yet I didn't know how. I couldn't teach school . . . or anythin'." Her voice faded, and the green eyes blurred with tears.

Barbara blinked back her own. She remembered the first time she had met Nance and the fear she'd seen lurking in the girl's face. Now she knew the story behind the fear.

"Nancy," she began softly, "if God has forgiven your ugly past, and you know He has, don't you think Ed could forgive, too? I know your Aunt Mame has."

Nance shook her head wildly. "I haven't told Ed about . . . about my baby and all the rest. I couldn't tell him. He'd hate me forever!"

"But why?"

"Oh, Barbara, don't you see that I oughtn't even breathe the same air as Ed Curtis, much less tell him about my past? It must'a been hard enough for God to forgive me. Then for Ed—"

"The Bible says 'as far as the east is from the west so far has he removed our transgressions from us.' God loves us unconditionally. If Ed is worthy to preach the Gospel, he will surely have read what the Bible says about it!"

Nance buried her head in her arms again and began to weep. Barbara sat by silently and waited as her sobbing continued. *Oh, Lord, what can I tell her to show her that Your love never fails? And that Ed must know that, too?*

Suddenly Nance pulled out a crumpled lacy handkerchief and quickly wiped her tears away. She jumped to her feet and started for the door. "I . . . gotta go now." Her face looked stricken. "It's no use."

As she started for the door, Willie barreled into the room at that moment and almost knocked her down as they collided. He drew back with a startled exclamation.

"Oh, Nance, I didn't see you!" He gently held her arm as she steadied herself and he asked, "Somethin' botherin' ya?"

Barbara and Nance looked at each other, and Barbara nodded. "Willie, Nance Drubeck's trying to avoid a certain young man who loves her. She loves him, too, but says she isn't worthy of Ed Curtis. Do you believe her?"

Willie pushed back his cap and grinned. "Ya mean, she ain't sure if God's forgiven her? Well, if Jesus could forgive the woman at the well, why wouldn't God forgive Nance?" He turned toward Nance. "If God forgives, it's done, once and for all. That settles it. Besides, Ed Curtis knows all about her havin' the baby and all the other stuff."

Nance's eyes widened as if thunderstruck. "Who . . . who told him? Did you?"

Willie laughed uproariously. "Not me! Everybody in town knows about it. Sure. He came into the lumberyard the other day lookin' for a piece of wood for Clell to fix the broken porch railin' at the hotel. He told me he'd knowed about Nance all the time, and if she loved him, that was all that mattered. Did you know he used to be a barkeep and a gambler before he became a Christian?"

Nance's green eyes grew wider with shock. "Ed Curtis? Oh

. . . You mean God could still use him to bring the good news of salvation . . . after all that?"

Willie nodded. "That's exactly right, Nance."

"But—"

"So what's keepin' ya from sayin' yes?"

"I know so little about the Bible," she began slowly, "although I've been readin' it every spare minute. Even Pastor Sternberg has been showin' me Scriptures to help me grow. I never knew that the Apostle Peter denied he knew Christ—three times! That . . . that's what happened before Christ was crucified. Ain't—isn't that somethin'?"

Barbara laid a hand on Nance's shoulder. "Yes, Nancy. Yet Peter became one of the boldest men for the cause of Christ after he learned Christ had forgiven him. And you can count on Ed to help you grow in faith."

Nance stood in the doorway hesitantly. "Then . . . then you think I should tell Ed I'll marry him?"

"It's your decision. It's between you and God, Nancy."

A bright smile suddenly lit the stricken face into radiant beauty, and she started toward the door again.

"I'll do it. Yes, I'll do it!" Then she hurried down the steps and quickly untied the horse from the hitching post.

"Don't forget to invite us to the weddin'!" Willie yelled after her.

As the buggy clattered down the lane, Barbara turned to Willie with a tired smile. "When we first came to Ellsworth, Nance . . . Nancy was about the first person I met. I must confess that I wanted to help her, for Mame's sake, at first. Only, she didn't want to be helped and I almost gave up. But I saw deep fear in her eyes then. Sometimes it's hard to understand God's ways, Willie."

"Well, all we know is—He knows what He's doin'."

A tear slid down Barbara's cheek and she brushed it away with the corner of her apron. "Willie, I never thought I'd say this, but I'll miss Nancy when she and Ed leave."

Willie folded his arms and stared at her. "This town ain't been too kind to us since we moved here, with the riffraff, the cattle trouble and the dust and everythin'. But I guess God still wanted us here. You was to help Nance, ya know. Don't you think so?"

"Has the Lord planned for us to be here, in spite of all the trials that have overwhelmed us?" she responded pensively as they both stared out the bare window at the empty lane where Nance's buggy had disappeared moments ago.

For my ways are not your ways, says the Lord . . .

The words sifted over her like a gentle rain and Barbara smiled through her tears. *Lord, use me wherever You can!*

CHAPTER 22

*A*week later, Nancy Drubeck and Ed Curtis were married at a quiet wedding ceremony in the Old Reliable's shabby parlor. When Barbara had offered the use of their new home for the occasion, Nance declined, saying, "It's in the Ol' Reliable where the Lord found me. Besides, Aunt Mame insists her cookin's bettern' yours! And she's the only family I've got." Her voice trailed away, and Barbara suspected tears lurking in the soft green eyes.

The harsh noises of clattering cookware and table service echoed through the hotel when Barbara and Charlie arrived with their family that morning for the 11 o'clock wedding. The handful of guests seated on the parlor's shabby chairs awaiting the wedding pair was a motley collection of women looking rather pathetic in their coarse and faded dresses. Barbara suspected some were prostitutes. Around them, a few chubby children fidgeted and fussed.

Barbara looked at her own carefully mended blue gingham that had seen so many scrubbings and eyed her two sons sharply. She had given them strict orders to behave, with dire promises of consequences if they didn't. Sally Ann smelled fresh and clean in her pink smocked dimity which had come from Bitsy's boxes of "out-growns." When Barbara had demurred, Bitsy's rejoinder was, "A professor's family is expected to dress like city folks. You might as well use them!"

Charlie sat beside her, looking uncomfortable in his best starched, but mended, white shirt and slicked-back dark curls that tumbled over his forehead. Willie sprawled beside the boys, his lanky legs stretched out. He flashed a grin at Barbara, as though underpinning her staunch encouragement of Nance's eventual decision to marry Ed Curtis.

Mame was gaudy and resplendent in a loud, purple and cerise figured dress that hung shapelessly over her large figure. Her gray hair was bunched in a skimpy bun at the nape of her neck. She pattered from the kitchen into the parlor and sat down in the front row.

"I'm next of kin," she whispered huskily to Barbara as she leaned back, tugging at the flamboyant skirt that crept up almost to her knees.

Barbara knew Mame had outdone herself in preparing the wedding meal, and that everything was under control in the hotel's large, greasy kitchen. Naturally, she was still her same gritty self, even in her wedding day "finery."

Just then there was a sudden flurry as Nance stepped through the open doorway, followed by the tall, smiling bridegroom, and began walking slowly toward the pastor. Her simple, starched, white cotton frock with a ruching of lace around the neckline had a full, tucked skirt which fit her beautifully. Her silky brown hair was piled on top of her head with a sprig of tiny, yellow ironweed blooms behind her ear. Barbara caught her breath sharply, for she had never expected Nance Drubeck to be such a beautiful bride.

Ed Curtis, tall and lean in his dark gray trousers and light tweed coat, with his sandy hair freshly combed, stepped up beside her. Pastor Sternberg, wearing a black suit, stood before them with his open Bible.

"Dearly beloved, we are gathered here in the presence of God and these witnesses . . ."

Barbara remembered hers and Charlie's strange wedding vows some eight years ago, when Quaker Elder Buck, in his squeaky boots, intoned solemnly: "Does thee, Barbara

Temple, take Charles Warren . . . to be faithful on the Santa Fe Trail and on the wide plains . . ." and she stifled a little smile. Charlie reached over and pressed her hand. His summer blue eyes were shining.

After the ceremony, Mame ushered the wedding guests into the small dining room where the tables were set with fine hand-painted china, cut crystal, and sterling silver. She began to serve thick steaks, heaping mounds of mashed potatoes, bowls of buttered corn and little apple tarts smothered in cream—lots of good cooking from iron pots—plus real coffee.

Looking at the bride and groom, Barbara saw the love that shone in their eyes, and unbidden tears filled her own. Then she remembered how hard and sassy Nance had seemed the day she had rushed out of Nick Lent's Saloon, and how angry she was at Barbara's offer to help. She shook her head slightly and thought, *The change is astounding!* The wonder of God's love and grace and mercy had never failed to amaze her.

The twelve o'clock train sounded its long eerie blast outside on the tracks in the plaza. Ed jumped up from the table and grabbed Nance's arm.

"That's our train! We must hurry before it leaves without us."

Mame rushed up with Nance's neatly mended cape and as she flung it around the slim shoulders, her tears flowed freely.

Barbara, clutching Sally Ann in her arms, hurried up to the couple. She hugged the bride as her own tears cut shiny paths down her cheeks.

"Goodbye . . . Nancy," she wept softly. "You'll never know . . ." She couldn't go on.

"Oh, Barbara, *you'll* never know how much you meant to me. I've never really told you," Nance whispered huskily. "If you hadn't cared like you did . . . Oh, God loved me through you. I know that now."

"But I—"

"No, Barbara," she repeated. "In spite of my stubbornness, you didn't give up. Thank God, you didn't!"

Charlie took the fretting baby from Barbara's arms and went

out the door ahead of her.

After a few hasty goodbyes, Ed Curtis rushed the new Mrs. Curtis through the door and piloted her down the street. The conductor was standing in the doorway of the day coach as he swung the last of their bags into the car. Barbara watched as Nance stepped aboard with broadly beaming Ed at her heels.

Standing on the wooden walk across from the depot, Barbara and Mame, with their arms around each other, saw the train move slowly out of the station and pick up speed. Barbara continued to watch silently as the train became only a moving speck. Now the platform was deserted, except for the trainmen who were finishing their duties.

A great wave of loss rolled over her, as though another chapter of her life was definitely closed.

Mame blew her nose loudly and brushed the tears from her florid face. Her gaudy dress looked wilted and damp. "Well, Barb'ra, whoever would'a known the part you'd play in makin' a respectable woman outta my niece! God never took His hand off your shoulder, did He? Now I gotta get back to mindin' my own business with Cady Benson," and she began to amble back to the hotel.

Charlie beckoned to Barbara. It was time to head back to the ranch. She knew he had taken enough time away from his work to see Nancy Drubeck and Ed Curtis safely married.

In the days that followed the wedding, Barbara's sense of loss persisted. Mame's reminder of the ex-gambler made her uneasy. *I should be grateful for our home,* she told herself. *After all, if it weren't for Cady, we wouldn't have been able to move into this spacious limestone house.* Charlie's words of reassurance came back to her—"Mame's a shrewd woman, and she knows what she's doing." Yes, the gritty woman always seemed to know where she was headed.

As the days passed, suddenly there were no cattle markets with the collapse of the New York Stock Exchange. The cattle that were left were pushed farther west to graze on what dry shriveled tufts of grass they could find.

Obviously, some Texas herds were still waiting, hoping the

market would open a bit. But Charlie was worried. Without the cattle trade, the railroads faced being shut down or would pass into receivership. With their own herd suffering from the drought, what would the future hold for their ranch?

Day after day the dry winds whirled and shrieked in a smothering dust-blowing hell. Barbara squinted into the pale sky, then glanced at the pitiful dwindling stacks of shucked corn in the field north of the house. She wondered how many more days of drought the pastures could stand. The immeasurable, everlasting wind that had given the state its name, which meant "people of the south wind, " was another good reason why anyone would be crazy to live in this seemingly God-forsaken place.

Ever since the summer, it had been blowing the fine dust from the fields, slipping it under the doors and around windows and settling it on tables and bedcovers.

One day Willie had come home by mid-morning saying that most businesses in town had closed for the day.

"There ain't much trade goin' on, anyway. We was s'pose to haul lumber out four miles north of town where they're buildin' the new country school, but it's too dusty. That's where Danny will go when it's finished."

"Can I go see it, Momma? Can I?" Danny pulled at Barbara's sleeve.

Barbara shut the door firmly. "Most assuredly not today, son! Wait until you can see something outdoors. As long as I can teach you at home—"

"But I wanna go to school with other boys!" he wailed. "When will it be ready, Uncle Willie? When?"

Willie shook his head. "Maybe by Christmas, if the weather holds out. Just be patient."

Dirt surged as the whistling wind picked up. A weird blue-green sky hovered over the barns, and by noon the wind started to tumble in high billows, flinging up clods into its maw. It seemed to roll over everything.

Then it hit—total, utter darkness, and smothering silence, with only the hiss of twisting silt in the background.

Pitchers of milk turned black, ducks and geese flew terrified, and jack rabbits staggered blindly across the lane. Windows turned ebony as Barbara fumbled in the darkness to light the lamps.

She picked up the fretting Sally Ann and bedded her down in the crib after she had wiped the grimy face with a wet cloth. *Where were the boys?* They needed wet towels for their faces to keep from breathing dust.

"Jem? Danny?" she called anxiously. They had played upstairs all morning.

Jem came downstairs, his face black as soot. "What you want, Momma?" he muttered.

"Where's Danny? Here, let me give you some wet towels for your faces, then go back upstairs until this blows over!"

"Danny's not here."

"Isn't here? What do you mean?" she asked, her voice harsh. "He's got to be. Surely he—"

"He said he wanted to see the 'koolhouse," Jem said in a small voice. "He wanted me to go with him, but I didn't want to go outside. Too dirty."

"Outside! Danny went out?" Fear swept through her. "Willie—" Barbara screamed, tearing through the house in search of her brother-in-law.

Willie slammed into the kitchen. "I made sure the horses were all right, and closed the cattle sheds."

"Was Danny with you?"

"Sure didn't see him. He ain't here?"

Barbara felt the blood drain from her face. "I can't find him! Jem says he wanted to see the schoolhouse. He could've been gone before the total darkness hit. Oh, Willie! What shall we do? Where's Charlie?" Panic dragged at her and slowed her footsteps. *Oh, dear Lord, please look after Danny.*

"I'm sure Charlie will come home after the storm lets up, so don't worry about him. About Danny—"

"What shall we do, Willie? He . . . Danny's so small. If he's out there in this blinding dust . . . I must find him." She stumbled toward the door.

Willie grabbed her shoulders. "You stay right here! Let me see what I can do, although it's black as night out there. You can't see your nose in front of your face."

"But Willie, I can't just stay here!"

"Yes, you can. You stay and pray, and I'll go find him."

With that, he pulled on his cap and disappeared into the darkness.

CHAPTER 23

*B*arbara crouched down on the floor, her arms cradling her head as she began to weep. Had God forsaken them this time? Surely He had forgotten them in the once-promising Smoky Hill Valley. If Danny's life was snuffed out in this black blizzard, how could she handle the loss?

She recalled the winter of '65 when she had stayed late at the schoolhouse at Marion Centre after the teacher had left. Low, scudding clouds had blown in from the northwest rolling over the prairies spitting sleet and snow. As she had cowered against the blizzard when she set out for the trail to Uncle Daniel's cabin, the strong wind and raging sleet had wrapped itself around her. Snow had whirled into her eyes and nostrils as needles of ice cut her face. She couldn't see a thing as she stumbled along.

Was it any worse than this choking blackness that now whipped and billowed across the plains? Danny and Willie, too, were out there, somewhere in this blinding whirlwind of dust. Her grueling nightmare of '65 had returned.

Tears gushed amid her harsh and angry sobs and streaked through the thick dust that covered her hands and face.

She cried aloud, "God, oh God, why have You done this to me? To us? To take away those so dear to me now—my son, Willie." Fear gripped her as panic filled her voice, "Perhaps even Charlie is in danger if he started home in the middle of this storm. It's all so unfair!" she sobbed.

A hollow feeling thrummed inside of her as it had the time she had received the news of Matthew Potter's death. She felt trapped by the wandering trails that had crossed her life leading to unknown places that seemed to lead to nowhere.

Again she was reminded of the time she'd been caught in that white blizzard, and how Ezra and Mehitabel Foster, former slaves, had taken her into their crude stone hut and had warmed and fed her. She had been so sure she wouldn't survive that blizzard at Marion Centre, but she had.

She heard their words again. *"Your stew's getting cold . . . God loves you and so does we." They had made a difference! Does God really want me to make a difference, too? Hadn't He used me to show Nance Drubeck to the Lord? God had really cared. He wouldn't forsake us now!*

Just then she grew aware that all was quiet outside, with only a thin whisper of silt hissing under the eaves.

This too shall pass . . .

She got to her knees and placed her arms on the windowsill. The massive, rolling wave of dirt that had boiled and tumbled over the prairie had grown stagnant and still.

Then she thought she heard voices. They were faint shouts at first, becoming more distinct with high-pitched words.

"Sorry . . . I didn't know."

"But you were plain stupid, boy!" snapped a strong, gravelly voice. "I hope you'll never—"

The door burst open as Willie pushed Danny inside the house. Barbara stumbled toward him and threw her arms around him. In the brown pall of the dim lamplight, she hugged him tightly. He looked so contrite, so sorry, and she pushed back his dirt-encrusted hair and kissed him over and over.

With a sudden shake of her head, she pulled him into the kitchen. "Let's wash your face, son. I must make sure it's really Daniel Charles Warren under all that dirt!"

Danny laughed out loud, then clung to Barbara's waist with

tears choking his words, "I . . . I'm so sorry, Momma . . . I wanted to see the school. But the storm came so quick, so I lay down in the ditch. It got awful dark and I cried."

Barbara looked at Willie, who coughed and nodded, then took up the story. "I still don't know what happened. I have no idea where I was or where he was. Just then the storm stopped, almost sudden-like. And without knowin' where I was goin', I stumbled along, callin' his name. I made out the ditch and somethin' moved. It was Danny. If you want me to give him a good lickin' for the trouble he caused—"

"That won't be necessary. God was good, and He directed your steps, Willie. Thank you for going out there in that storm. Hasn't it happened over and over? In spite of all the snags we've hit, God is still in control. But we're so prone to forget." Barbara swallowed tears of gratitude. She was sure Charlie, too, would be home before long. *Yes, I can trust in the Lord,* she reminded herself.

Gradually, the heavy brown pall lifted, and although it still hung over the day, she believed the worst was over.

Willie had gone for the broom and began to scoop up the thick layer of dust that covered the floor, while Barbara pumped a bucket of water and began to scrub the dirt from the table and chairs.

It was time to fix supper.

CHAPTER 24

*T*he wind died down over the next few days, and slowly the dust settled. The dry air was at a standstill and dirt was piled up everywhere. Fields were swept bare of topsoil, yet not a blade of dry grass moved. Even the Smoky Hill River was choked with silt.

The air of late October grew brittle with frost. Thin, hungry cattle stood hunched on the south sides of the sheds in dumb, stolid misery. The dust storm had culled out the weakest from several herds. Cows began milling around, bawling for water and horning each other into the rail fences.

Each day after work, Charlie and Willie hauled water to the watering holes from the well beside the house. It seemed the cool streams that gushed from the pump were endless in spite of the drought. Some ranchers had been forced to dig deeper wells to reach the underground water levels that hadn't been depleted.

Barbara scanned the horizon for rain clouds, but the hazy, blue skies were bare. She moved about silently, often deep in thought about their future, as she prepared the meals for the family. Charlie's work on the railroad held out as other products were shipped to the eastern markets, along with a few cattle, for whatever price they would bring. Mame seldom came out for her unpredictable visits, and Barbara felt lonely again, since few folks cared to socialize, it seemed.

"I wonder if Nance and Ed made it safely to Oregon?" she mused aloud one afternoon as Willie stepped into the kitchen for a drink of fresh water. "Believe it or not, I miss that girl."

"Yeah. She was quite a character," Willie said, running a finger over the dusty windowsill. It was impossible to keep the house dust-free. "But I'm glad you did what you could for her. If you hadn't kept after her about God lovin' her—"

"And if you hadn't told her that Ed's past wasn't so savory either—"

The looked at each other and grinned.

"Well, it all goes to show God knows what He's doin'," he added as he picked up his cap and started for the door.

Barbara sighed. "We felt so sure He wanted us here at Ellsworth. But with all that's happened here, now with the dust and drought, Willie, do you suppose things will ever change?"

"Haven't they already? Look, the poker and boozin' has stopped. Oh, sure, there's still a few places, but things has settled down considerably."

"But the dry, dusty weather, Willie. How will our ranch survive?"

Willie shrugged his shoulders. "I know. I ain't hankered for all that either, but ain't there a place in the Bible that talks about God's faithfulness, His mercies, and that we ain't to be consumed, because His compassions don't fail?"

Barbara nodded slowly. "You're right. 'Great is thy faithfulness.'" She picked up the Bible from the lamp table and paged through it until she found Lamentations chapter 3. Then she continued reading: " 'Let us search and try our ways, and turn again to the LORD. Let us lift up our heart with our hands unto God in the heavens.' Willie, as you say, we must believe God knows what He's doing."

She turned to the stove as Willie went out of the kitchen. Why was it so hard to trust when things went wrong? *Lord, give me reasons to praise You today.* It was a prayer from her heart.

If all went according to schedule, Willowbrook Schoolhouse would be finished before Christmas. They had decided Danny could continue his education there with the other children, but he would have a mile long walk each day to the north. The schoolhouse was rather crude and rough, since it had been constructed by the hands of volunteers to keep costs down. Still, it was good to know their children would be schooled. Even now, Danny talked of the time when he could help with the cattle. Already his special project was a wobbly little black calf Charlie had given him.

"Now that you're seven years old, Danny," Charlie said solemnly, "it's time you take some responsibility."

Yes, the children were growing up fast. Barbara reminded herself to take joy in her children in spite of their problems. Jem would turn four in a few months, and even Sally Ann was already pulling herself to her feet when a chair was convenient. The children and the work kept Barbara busy and eased her loneliness.

Mame came out the next afternoon and set a jar of sandhill plum jelly on the table.

"Here. I didn't think you knowed how to cook jams and jellies, Barb'ra," she said tartly. "Jams don't cook good in enameled pans, you know," she added in her usual tactless way.

Barbara bit her lower lip as she set the jar on the kitchen shelf. "Well, of course, I haven't had the experience in the kitchen that you have. But whatever you fix always tastes better than what I cook."

Mame plunked herself into a chair and stretched out her plump legs in front of her. "True enough. Good thing I'm still here. But I can't say how much longer I'll be around."

Barbara whirled away from the work table where she was stirring up the inevitable batch of cornbread. "Are you leaving? Where will you go, Mame? I thought your job at the hotel kitchen was secure. Is it because Nance is gone?"

"It ain't that. I'm jest gettin' tired of always cookin' vittles for other folks. Guess I done it for too long. Cady's been beggin' me to marry him. But I dunno—" She shrugged her plump shoulders. "He's headin' East before Christmas. He's plenty well fixed and I wouldn't have to work so hard for my keep. I'm really tempted."

"But Mame—"

"I know what you're thinkin'. Cady ain't a believer in the Lord, and that bothers me, too. Well, I ain't promised him yet. The Lord will have to work that out in His own way."

All evening Barbara's mind scratched and fretted about Mame and her situation. True, Cady was a handsome man, tall and muscular, with twinkling blue eyes, sandy hair, a neat handle bar mustache. Although he had made a lot of money as a gambler, he vowed to give up the vice, according to Mame. *She's a sensible woman,* Barbara reminded herself, *but tired of "cookin' vittles" for others, she says. Lord, please lead Mame in the right way,* she prayed silently.

As November trembled with cold winds, the dry earth crackled with frost. The hoped-for rains had not come, and spirits in Ellsworth County flagged. Charlie came home after work and fed the cattle the skimpy rations of shriveled hay, for the lowland meadow to the west had yielded a fair crop of fodder. Then wearily he tumbled into bed after the evening meal.

Willie, too, dragged home from the lumberyard and went to bed soon after supper, with the daylight hours fading. It was as though every person, every living being in the county had lost their zest for living. Barbara had all she could do to push herself with cleaning, cooking, mending, washing and looking after the children. She knew that the drought hit all over Kansas and other areas of the Midwest, and everyone was effected by it. Although she sometimes wondered if they should move again, she realized it probably wouldn't be different anywhere else.

Since mid-November the smoky pall of prairie fires had hung over the prairies to the west. Night after night the skies lit up with grass fires in one direction or another.

One morning about 10 o'clock, Barbara saw a brownish,

copper-colored cloud roll from the hills to the southwest, boiling up for an instant at one point, then another. With alarm, she realized the prairie fire had rolled perilously near the ranch, on the opposite side of the Smoky Hill River. She stood anxiously on the porch and watched.

Suddenly Charlie was there, and was hitching the teams to the plow. "To the cellar! Get the children to the cellar!" he shouted. Then he jammed the plow into ground and started the team in a circle.

Barbara turned and ran into the house and shepherded the children into the cellar under the house, where she put Danny in charge. As she scrambled back upstairs, the smell of burning grass grew stronger in the air. For a moment she watched Charlie from the kitchen door, then she grabbed empty burlap sacks from the shed and began to soak them in water. Charlie shook his head fiercely when he saw her.

"How about the cattle?" she yelled as she saw the team trembling with fright at the smell of fire and smoke, and the roar of the rising wind. The cows bellowed, and the rest of the horses snorted and ran nervously back to the pasture as he continued to plow the fire guard around the buildings.

The sun had grown dim with the flying dust and smoke when Charlie shouted to her. "Get down to the cellar, Barbara, where you'll be safe!"

"But Charlie—"

"I said, get down to the cellar!"

With the wind whipping her skirts about her, she hurried down the stone steps where Jem was crying and Danny, trying his best to console him.

"The fire can't get in this stone house," Danny yelled while Jem shrieked with fright.

The baby whimpered in her basket, and Barbara picked her up and laid her gently across her shoulder.

"Danny's right. The house won't burn," she soothed. "I'm thankful for this stone house."

For an hour the wind blew without stopping. Occasional lulls were followed by blasts that seemed to shake the foundations of the house. Barbara tried to find ways to occupy the boys to keep them from worrying about their father outside, and she prayed. Gradually the wind died into small fitful gusts. By two o'clock it was quiet.

Barbara went up the steps and looked out cautiously, the baby asleep on her shoulder. The sun shone with a sickly light through the dust and smoke that lingered in the air, and she told the boys to come up, too.

Charlie came toward the house, his face covered with soot and dust. He drew off his hat and wiped his forearm over his face, leaving a dirty smear on his shirt sleeve. His dark curls tumbled over his forehead and he pushed them back absently.

"The fire's stopped," he said wearily. "It stayed on the other side of the Smoky Hill. That's what saved us."

Barbara nodded, and noticed how weary he looked. Then she said, "What made you decide to come home?"

"When we saw it coming, we were to make sure the railroad ties didn't catch fire, but other hands told me to go home and make sure our place was safe. They promised to handle the railroad right-of-way since there are rocks along the tracks and the danger was less. Remember the prairie fire when we lived near Fort Larned?"

She smiled. "I'll never forget it. It was that fire guard you plowed that saved our soddy."

"That, and your prayers!"

"That's why I got the burlap sacks. I wanted to help stomp out the fire. I wonder if the fire reached the town?"

Charlie stared at her with a stark frown. "Barbara, I don't know why we ever decided to move to this God-forsaken place. I must've been insane to drag you and the children out here."

Just then Willie rode up on his horse. His soot-covered face was framed in a merry grin. Willie, always cheerful, was like good medicine.

"Willie!" Barbara cried. "What on earth makes you so happy? The town—"

"We saved it, but it took everyone workin' hard to do it. I just wondered if ya noticed that black smudge in the west."

Through the murky haze it was barely visible, but then Barbara saw the unmistakable thunderheads. Already flashes of lightning split the sky. Sally Ann stirred restlessly. Rain clouds! This time they were real.

The storm, when it broke, came in a fury of wind and rain, lashing against the limestone house and rattling the windows. Everything dripped and splashed and wept. The panes streamed with water as sheet after sheet of glittering wetness swept across the prairies. Rain at last!

The sweet, fresh smell of wet earth was like incense, and as the rain settled into a steady downpour, she called the boys out on the porch to watch. For one hour it poured from gray skies.

The rain had cooled the air and Barbara shivered. She breathed the soft baby-smell of the chubby child who relaxed against her, and went into the house and laid her in the crib and tucked a blanket over her.

A small sharp gust of wind swirled wet drops against the window pane and thrust clammy fingers around the edges of the glass. A tendril of ivy Barbara had nursed and coaxed, twisted and turned near the stone walls. As suddenly as it had come, the rain was over.

The rain clouds began to break as thin, pink sunlight filtered through the torn white clouds.

Barbara drew a deep, satisfying breath. After all the dry, dreary weeks, the Lord had answered their prayers for rain. As if to assure her of God's gentle peace, the yellow cowslip prairie moon swung up over the east and scattered gold magic over the freshly-washed earth. *Great is Thy faithfulness,* she recalled.

With a heart full of praise, Barbara called the boys into the house and began to prepare supper.

CHAPTER 25

$\mathcal{A}$ tantalizing breeze blew through the cool November morning on uneven wads of fog that were left after last night's rain. Then the sun edged over the rim of the world. Low arches of the hills flanked the Smoky Hill River that sang between muddy banks. A brisk fire burned and snapped in the grate of the wood stove, shedding warmth throughout the cozy kitchen.

Barbara stood in the doorway and watched a large roan clopping up the muddy lane pulling an unfamiliar buggy. When it drew to a stop at the hitching post, she recognized Cady Benson. His gray felt hat was pulled over his sandy hair, and it shaded his neatly-trimmed, handle bar mustache. His fine leather jacket was open at the throat as he came up the porch. Rather hesitantly, Barbara invited him in.

"I came to see how the ranch fared in yesterday's prairie fire, and the rainstorm of last night," he said in his smooth, clipped voice. "But I see you all survived. Everything looks fine."

"Yes, thank God," she said, pulling out a chair and motioning him toward it. "Charlie worked hard to save the ranch buildings. Fortunately the fire didn't jump across the river. Then the rain came."

"Yes, and it looks like we can expect more of the same," he said as he looked at the clouds to the west. "I'm very pleased with the way Charlie has handled things, and since I'm going away in a few days I wanted to be sure the ranch was in good hands. I couldn't be more pleased."

"You're leaving, Mr. Benson?"

"Back to Boston, where I have other business investments."

"You're going—alone?"

He drew a long breath. "Not if I can persuade Mame Probst to go with me! She's still holding out. I know she isn't a raving beauty and she's rather snappish if her dander's up, which is often! But she's a great cook, a most interesting companion—never boring. She'd not lack for anything."

After Cady was gone, Barbara was left with a feeling of desolation. *Cady's such a charmer, he'll surely persuade Mame to say "yes,"* Barbara worried. But Mame seemed intent on marrying a Christian, so it just didn't add up.

After the refreshing rain, the whole world brightened, it seemed. If the rains continued, the chances for good crops would enhance their prospects of a better future on their ranch. But if Mame left, Barbara would be lonely again. In spite of the woman's gruff exterior, she had been a faithful, dear friend. How would they have survived the past six months without the big, bouncy woman?

With a sigh, Barbara turned to her work. Danny would enroll in the new country school by the end of the week, and she must see that his few clothes were patched and clean.

She had recently become better acquainted with some of the women in church. It would take the edge off her loneliness, she decided, to accept Mary Rossford's invitation to a quilting bee this afternoon. *Of course, I don't know how to quilt,* she told herself, *but it's time I learned. Some day I'll invite the ladies to this house.* It was one of the most elegant homes in the community. Although it lacked the finesse, the charm and expert workmanship of the southern plantation homes, it was probably the closest she'd ever get to living in one. She smiled at the prospect of inviting guests.

The boys had been denied the companionship of friends in town for so long, and this outing would be good for them all.

After she harnessed the team, she buttoned Sally Ann into Jem's outgrown coat and made sure the boys were warm in their wool caps and jackets. After fastening the hooks along the long, tucked waist of her old pink checked gingham and pulling on her shabby coat, Barbara herded the boys out to the wagon while she carried the baby on her left hip, slamming the kitchen door behind her.

The cold wind had died down, but the freshness of the newly washed earth exhilarated her.

"We'll spend the best part of the afternoon at the Rossfords, then hurry home," she told the boys after they had settled into the wagon's back seat and she had tucked the blankets around them and the baby. "I hope you'll play nicely with Johnny Rossford and the Beecher boys," she said stoutly, clucking to the team.

"Yeah, but Billy Beecher got ants," three-year-old Jem sniffed.

"Ants? What do you mean, ants?" Barbara asked, raising her voice above the squishy noise of the team on the muddy road.

"He caught a bunch of red ants in a jar and feeds them corn," Danny snorted. "He said in Sunday school after we learned the 'Go, thou sluggard' verse, that it's a sure sign we'll have a good school year 'cause ants work hard."

"You'll have a good school year with or without ants," Barbara said tartly.

While pulling into the long, muddy lane of the Rossford farm, Barbara focused her attention on the gray clapboard walls of the shabby square house and drab barns. She stopped at the front gate.

When they came in, the warm kitchen spilled over with children who had come along to spend the afternoon, and the boys soon rushed off to play. Mary Rossford ushered Barbara into the tiny parlor. The four other women, who were dressed no better than she was in shabby ginghams and faded percales, sat around the half finished quilt.

"I . . . I've never learned to quilt," Barbara apologized, after plump, teenaged Tina Rossford had relieved her of Sally Ann and she sat down at the quilt. "But I decided it was time I mingle with the church women."

"Yes, and catch up with the latest news," pert little Arabella Beecher chirped, looking up from the gaily-patched quilt as she squinted to thread her needle.

"You mean gossip!" Faith Ballard chuckled with a toss of her bright head. "Which reminds me—I hear Mame Probst is gettin' married."

"Married? Who to?" Mary asked.

"Well, of course, *you* know." Arabella paused, arching one eyebrow sagely.

Faith chuckled. "What a surprise! Who'd have thought she'd wind up with *him*? And how he'll ever put with *her*."

Barbara's heart sank. *So it was true. Mame was going to marry Cady Benson. And everyone knew it but me.* She shut her ears to the other gossip that flew as busily as the needles around the gaudy quilt. *This is going to take some getting used to,* she decided. *Maybe I should've stayed home.*

But the boys needed to play with their friends, and she didn't have the heart to get up and leave, especially when she noticed Mary serving generous squares of gingerbread with dollops of whipped cream on top and barley coffee in crockery cups. As she enjoyed the refreshments, she learned that the Beecher boys would pass by the lane leading to their ranch on the way to school each morning. So she ventured to ask Mrs. Beecher if Danny might walk with them when he began attending the new school, too. They both agreed it would be a good idea since it was a long walk.

The afternoon was waning, so Barbara corraled her boys, picked up the baby and said her goodbyes. Sally Ann fretted all the way home while Danny and Jem discussed Billy Beecher's ants in their shrill voices. Barbara tried to tune them out.

She had just stabled the horses and put Sally Ann to bed for a late afternoon nap when Mame's horse fractured the muddy lane. Barbara welcomed her somewhat timorously, for the big, bulky woman looked every inch the radiant bride.

"Well, I said 'yes', and I know it's the best decision I ever made!" she bubbled as soon as she had jerked off her wraps.

I don't want to hear this, Barbara decided, *but I'd better get it from her straight.*

"You mean, you're going to marry Cady Benson after all?"

"Cady?" Mame shook her head. "He may be a good landlord, but he don't know my God."

"But who—?"

"Clell Dobbs." Mame chuckled. "S'prised ya, didn't I? Like I s'prised everyone in town."

"C-Clell Dobbs!" Barbara stared at Mame in amazement. *Mame and Clell? Mame Probst and McClellan Dobbs? The dear, funny little druggist with the vibrant faith and the big, bossy, blurry Mame? It was incongruous! But maybe not.* Barbara felt like laughing aloud in relief. Trying to conceal her mirth she drew a deep breath.

"Y-yes, you did surprise me. I had no idea—"

"Oh, Clell ain't much for looks. Not nearly as nice-lookin' as Cady, but he's a good man. A God-fearin' man."

"So you won't be leaving Ellsworth then?"

"Oh, but we are. We'll move to Kansas City where Clell's been offered a job in a big pharmacy plant. It ain't so far that we can't come up on the train now and then. It also means I can stop cookin' vittles for a whole town full of folks. Sometimes my legs get frightfully tired. But when we come to visit, I'll take over the cookin' for you and give you a rest. If only you had an iron cookin' pot."

"I'll miss you, Mame," Barbara said with tears lurking in her lustrous blue eyes. "But I know you won't forget us. Still, I do wish I had one special friend," she added wistfully.

"You'll find someone," Mame nodded, her florid face somber. "You always have. I guess I'll miss you more'n anybody, Barb'ra. You was such a stubborn, prissy thing once, and I know you didn't always take to my bossin' very well. But the Lord'll send you another friend—whenever you need one."

After Mame left, Barbara let her tears flow. Coming to this rough frontier town, she'd felt alone until her concern for

Nance had added a new twist to her life in spite of frustrations. Then dear little White Lily helped fill the void until Mame came back into her life. Yes, the Lord had sent somebody when she had needed someone. Now they were all leaving, and she cried some more.

When she mentioned it to Charlie that night, he drew her in his arms and kissed her. "I know you felt alone for so long, but don't forget that the Bible says, 'The Lord giveth and the Lord taketh away. Blessed be the Name of the Lord.' And remember if the Lord's *given* before, He can *give* again. He always will. He's restored the land to us now, and He'll give you another friend, too. How was your day at the quilting bee?"

Barbara explained briefly what she learned, and how Danny would be able to walk with the Beecher boys to school. Charlie thought it was a good idea, and Barbara realized that something good had come from her time spent at the Rossfords.

Two days later, after Pastor Sternberg had married them in a quiet ceremony, Mame and Clell boarded the train for Kansas City. Mame looked about as elegant as possible in the gaudy purple and cerise dress with her hair arranged in a flouncy bun, offset by a pair of dangly gold earrings. Clell looked almost handsome in his best gray suit with a red bow tie under his clean-shaven chin. He had slicked back what was left of his hair, and the smile that wreathed his face was genuine.

Willie laughed under his breath after the train picked up speed and rattled down the tracks, carrying them toward Kansas City. "Clell looks like a cat that swallered a bird, with the feathers still ticklin' his craw," he chuckled. "But I really think they'll be happy. He's a good man, and I'll venture to say he's the kind that would let someone boss him around for a change."

Danny had begun attending the new country school. After his first week of school, he came home in a whirl of excitement.

"We're gonna have a Christmas program, Momma, and I'm

gonna sing a song. Isn't that something!"

"Very nice. What will you sing? The 'Little Baby in a Manger' song you sang last year at church?"

"Oh, no, Momma. I'm singing the 'Nowhere' song."

"The—'Nowhere' song?"

"You know—'No where, no where, no where, no where, born is the King of Israel.'"

Barbara choked back her laughter. Then she said, "It's 'Noel', Danny. It means 'a Christmas song'."

Danny looked at her with a startled frown. "Huh? Well, as long as it's a Christmas song, does it matter how you sing it?" His face brightened as he continued, "And we're gonna have a tree with popcorn and stars and candles hung all over it."

Willie, who had just come into the kitchen, tousled Danny's hair. "I'll bet it will be the prettiest tree in Kansas. Say, Danny have you checked your calf this afternoon? It's growin' faster than you!"

With a quick movement, Danny jerked on his jacket and scampered out of the house.

Barbara shook her head. "Danny's sure growing fast. To think he's in a real school. His teacher tells me he's reading in the third reader."

"Yep." Willie stopped to stretch himself. "You taught him just fine, like ya did me. And ya got to admit that in spite of all the troubles we've been through, the boys are doin' real good.

"I'd better help him check the rest of the stock. Danny's gonna be a good rancher one of these days." With that, he buttoned up his jacket and went out.

CHAPTER 26

*B*arbara smiled as she watched Willie walk out to the barn with Danny. Yes, the boys were growing up fast. But so was Willie. *He's just turned 20 and he's never looked finer,* she thought. His freckles had all but disappeared, and his appearance was becoming very manly. Barbara noticed how he was taking an interest in the girls at church. It was hard to conceive of Charlie's congenial young brother becoming romantically interested in anyone. The time would come when he would move out on his own. But right now, she wasn't ready to see him go.

Christmas was almost upon them. Although it would be meager, as usual, she anticipated a happier yuletide this year in the new house, with Willie safely returned to them.

The day before Christmas, Charlie rode slowly into the yard from work and she was puzzled by the carriage from the livery stable clattering up behind him. *Now, who in the world?* she wondered.

As the guests climbed out, Barbara gasped in both surprise and delight. It was Lucas and Callie Herrington and their brood! "Oh, dear Lord, thank You, thank You!" she whispered under her breath as she set Sally Ann on the floor, grabbed her jacket and rushed out the door. Yes, they were at her doorstep—the Herringtons!

Barbara never forgot Callie Briggs as she was back in 1866 when the two wagons had stopped by the sod house, with Callie's two children, Dolly and James, and expecting another child. And behind Callie had come Lucas Herrington, the tall, lean giant with the rusty beard, followed by his two children, Sarah Lynn and Nelson.

The two families had been headed for Colorado when Callie's husband, Thayne, had drowned while crossing the Missouri River. Mary Herrington, Callie's sister, had died in childbirth near Independence. The baby had died, too.

There had been nothing left to do but for Callie to travel on with Lucas and his youngsters. But Callie had felt awkward about being in a "family way," since Lucas would obviously have to deliver Callie's baby.

She remembered how Mame had stopped in that day with news of a circuit preacher who would hold a church service at the Probst dugout the next day. She managed to barge into the conversation and to brashly size up the situation, to Barbara's embarrassment. Then she proceeded to suggest that Callie and Lucas "oughta get hitched so she'd have a husbin' to deliver the young'un when it came."

And that's exactly what happened. Barbara had quickly pulled together an impromptu wedding at Mame and Henry's dugout. The two sets of cousins seemed very happy with the marriage of their parents.

Barbara had loved Callie from the beginning, and now it was so special to see them all again.

All these fond memories flashed through Barbara's mind as she hurried out to the carriage. Callie, tall and blond as ever, beamed when Barbara grabbed her and gave her a warm hug.

"Oh, Callie! God sent you just when I needed someone. I can't believe I'm not dreaming," she cried.

Callie drew off her shabby blue scarf and shook out her full gray skirt. "You can't imagine how wonderful it was to see Charlie at the train station when our train pulled in this afternoon. We didn't know you'd moved here. Charlie says you have a nice little family."

"Oh, yes! There's Danny who's seven. Jeremy, or Jem as we call him, is three. And our baby girl, Sally Ann. It's so good to see you again. Do come in."

Amid a jumble of greetings and chatter, Barbara led them inside. She tried to sort out the Briggs-Herringtons: Sarah Lynn was tall and slender, with beautiful brown eyes flecked with green, and silky brown hair that curled over her forehead. *She must be all of 20 now,* Barbara thought. Dolly, James and Nelson were in their teens.

"And this is Jason?" Barbara pointed to a duplicate of James. "The son you had at Lamar?"

"Yes. He's a real fine young'un. Guess he'll have fun with your boys," Callie replied with a smile as the three young boys scampered off to play. "Lucas has been a good father to my brood and a lovin' husband, so it's worked out real fine. It was so good of Mame Probst to suggest that we get married."

Yes, Mame's suggestions, usually incongruous, most often were good! Barbara thought.

Charlie was already helping Lucas unhitch the team. As Barbara ushered her guests into the large front room, she paused suddenly.

"How long will you be in Ellsworth? Of course, you'll stay with us again, won't you? This time, we have plenty of room."

"We planned to stay at the Drover's Hotel over Christmas, but then we must move on. We didn't want to be on the train on Christmas Day."

"Leaving so soon? But where are you going? I wish you'd settle here."

"We'd lost track of you after you left Fort Larned, you know. Lucas got word that he has work back in Illinois where we came from. We plan to move back on the farm his folks left him. It will be best for us all. His work at the mines was never very good, and when the silver ore petered out, we knew we had to leave. Back home seemed like the only place—and the best place." She smiled, "Yes, we'll spend Christmas with you."

Suddenly she laughed. "Here we were at the train station,

acting like a flock of chickens that didn't know one end from the other! And then we saw Charlie. He insisted we come home with him, and I'm so glad we did."

"So am I. It's only—" Barbara paused with a catch in her voice. "Mame Probst just moved away. Sometimes I think I'll never have one special friend who will stay."

"The Lord will always see that you have someone, Barbara."

Already the sun was slanting toward the west, trailing a necklace of pink-tinted clouds after it. Then the sky deepened to purple, and melted into the dull gray twilight. One ray of pale gold shimmered along the horizon and lost itself in the upper heavens like a promise of hope.

Quickly Barbara scurried into the kitchen to prepare supper with pretty Sarah Lynn behind her, who immediately set to work peeling the panful of potatoes while Dolly set the plates and flatware on the table.

As she fried huge slabs of fresh beef and boiled great pots of carrots and turnips, Barbara's heart sang. Perhaps the past year had been rough, yet there had been compensations. They had touched so many lives: Nance, Clell, Ed, Mame, White Lily and now again, Lucas and Callie and their brood.

Seated around the supper table, her heart swelled with joy to have these dear friends as guests in this rough-and-tumble community on Christmas Eve. They worked together, passing bowls and platters of the simple but satisfying food, laughing and chatting as though they had never been apart.

Barbara smiled as she noticed Willie's surreptitious glances roving toward the lovely Sarah Lynn, and saw the girl's soft blushes as she met his gaze shyly.

Tomorrow would be Christmas Day. Although some would say there was little to celebrate, from a commercial point of view, in this home, the true celebration of the human heart through knowing Christ as Savior and Lord would reverberate. Barbara knew it would be a very special occasion—just as she'd hoped.

The stars winked in the black sky as Barbara and Charlie went upstairs to their bedroom. Once again the yellow cowslip prairie moon beamed through the window at them as they lay in bed and talked of the past year—their hopes for a better future, the many setbacks that were now behind them, and how God had been in their lives all along.

They now had the beginnings of the ranch that Charlie had aspired to for so long, and in time it would prosper. The pastures were good and the house was wonderful. Their "family of boys" and a "girl to help her" had already begun. Here they would stay.

"Did you notice Willie could hardly keep his eyes off Sarah Lynn's face?" Charlie chuckled. "One of these days he'll want his own place. Our church is growing, too, and the rough element in town is smoothing out. Some day this will be a fine place to bring up our family."

"It's already begun. I know now that God will always give me another friend when I need one. To have you, Charlie, and our little family and Willie—" Tears coursed gently down her cheeks, and she let them fall. "Oh Charlie, I'm so happy!"

"Barbara, as it says in Genesis, 'While the earth remaineth, seedtime and harvest, cold and heat, summer and winter, and day and night shall not cease.' Let's thank God, Barbara, for His many special promises," he whispered huskily. As he slipped from under the covers and she knelt down with him, he added, "And even for the wandering trails, God has led us on to bring us to this time and place."

"Yes," Barbara added, "to this place where He has brought us—to this, our home, sweet home!"